PRODIGY

PRODIGY

A Novella

Nancy Huston

McArthur & Company

First published in Canada by McArthur & Company, 2000

Canadian Cataloguing in Publication Data

Huston, Nancy, 1953-
  [Prodige. English]
  Prodigy

Translation of: Prodige
ISBN 1-55278-154-2

I. Title. II. Title: Prodige. English

PS8563.U8255P7613 2000   C843'.54   C00-931343-5
PQ3919.2.H87P7613 2000

Composition and Design by *Michael P. Callaghan*
Cover by *Tania Craan*
Typeset at *Moons of Jupiter, Inc.* (Toronto)
Printed in Canada by *Transcontinental Printing Inc.*

McArthur & Company
322 King Street West, Suite 402
Toronto, ON, M5V 1J2

10 9 8 7 6 5 4 3 2 1

The Publisher would like to acknowledge the financial support of the Government of Canada through the Book Publishing Industry Development Program (BPIDP) for our publishing activities. The publisher further wishes to acknowledge the financial support of the Ontario Arts Council for our publishing program.

For, with, and thanks to
Yves Angelo

Without music, life would be a mistake.
NIETZSCHE

I do not like myself. Yes.
SVIATOSLAV RICHTER

SOFIA

Ah! Larissa's roses are doing well this year. So are her delphiniums. I can smell them from up here at my bedroom window. My dear daughter. She tries so hard. Makes such an effort.

I can hear her making an effort right now, at the piano. Same old fugue from the *Opus 106*. Technically daunting. She's been working on it for more than a month and still it won't flow, won't take on meaning beneath her fingertips.... No, that's not it. She can't get it right. *For the love of God*, she's saying to herself, *wasn't it written for human hands?* And, with a sigh of rage, she takes it from the top again.

Ah yes. I know Larissa's torments off by heart.

LARA

Sweating already. Sweating again. Rivulets of sweat trickling down my forehead and my back. I break off. Grab a pencil and ferociously note the fingering on the sheet music, knowing all the while that I'll disobey what I have written down, transgressing my own orders as soon as I get a chance. Then I throw myself back into it, running up against the wall of notes and trying to turn it into a wave. Failing. Falling. It's the end of all movement. The end of beauty and truth.

I'll never get there...

SOFIA

I'll never get there, she's saying to herself. I can hear each and every one of my Dochenka's thoughts. *The piano*, she's thinking, *is both what lets me and what keeps me from expressing myself.* Ah, if only she'd worry about expressing Beethoven, rather than herself!

Her whole body's tensed up. Bad for the child, very bad. I know Lara, she's feeling guilty. Well, what can you expect? She shouldn't have given up God. Those atheists — they think they're so clever! At least when you believe in God, you've got one great big, excellent reason for feeling guilty and there's an end to it, you don't need to keep fussing over it all the time.

LARA

Take a deep breath. Count to nine breathing out, just like in my obstetric yoga classes. I've got to calm down, be patient. Unclench my jaws. Relax my calf muscles. Breathe in, breathe out. Start over again. Okay, let's begin....

SOFIA

The doorbell rings. Ah! The call of duty. Now she has no choice — now she'll have to stop working on the fugue and give the redhead his lesson, yes, her best pupil, three o'clock, punctual as usual, accompanied by Mama as usual.... From up here at my bedroom window, I can see them waiting on the front steps.

Larissa comes to the door. Big smile, I'm sure of it. As if everything were just fine. My daughter knows she's attractive — at least she's got that much going for her. In fact she's quite beautiful. People describe her as radiant. The beauty of an eighteen-year-old girl can be intimidating, but a lovely, smiling woman in the full bloom of her thirties reassures people, warms their hearts.

"What marvellous roses! You can smell them blocks away!"

"Yes," says my daughter. "September roses have a headier fragrance than midsummer ones...."

Sitting at my open window, I watch everything that goes on, eavesdropping shamelessly. I don't even bother to hide. That's one nice thing about old age. There you are and no one gives a damn; it's as though you were transparent. Life agrees with me, and I take it as it comes.

"Oh, I really must apologize, Madame Mestral — I meant to attend your recital last Tuesday. I saw the posters, I even wrote it down in my datebook, and then.... You know how it is, what with school starting up again and all, I got swamped and it completely slipped my mind...."

"Please... don't mention it."

"I hope it went well? You were accompanying a mezzo-soprano.... Schumann *lieder*, wasn't it?"

"Yes, Schubert... that's right...."

Doesn't bat an eyelash. As if confusing Schumann and Schubert were nothing....

LARA

Stiff, straight, narrow, silent, eyes lowered behind the thick lenses of his glasses, Alexis clumsily edges around me and heads for the piano. He prefers to leave the ladies chattering behind him on the doorstep. I can understand that. He has no wish to put up with feminine effusions and effluvia. He starts his warm-up — major and minor scales and arpeggios, playing fast and loud. I'm always amazed at the contrast between his self-confidence at the keyboard and his shy, almost introverted behaviour in real life.

"So did you have a nice summer?" his mother murmurs now, in an annoyingly knowing tone of voice. "How are you feeling? Is everything going all right?"

"Yes, just fine, thanks."

"How far along are you now?"

"Five and a half months, nearly six."

"Just three months left to go."

"Mm-hm."

"I don't want to discourage you or anything, but... the worst is yet to come."

"Oh, I know, I know, don't worry!"

I burst out laughing in hopes that she'll shut up. I've always been shocked by the brutal intimacies which mothers indulge in with mothers-to-be. A sudden eruption of physicality, sex, and death in the most trivial conversations. So she knows that Robert and I made love six months ago. And that before long, my body will be a huge and heavy machine, a cruel bulldozer gone haywire, completely escaping my control, driving me mad with pain.... How dare she tell me the worst is yet to come? As if I didn't know....

And *why is it that — for me — everything is always so very hard?*

SOFIA

What a fuss French women make about giving birth. What sissies they are — it's perfectly shameful. We bit the belt and there was an end to it. Didn't spend months getting ready for the event, and more months recovering from it afterwards. Gymnastics classes reimbursed by the government! Never heard of anything so silly.... French women are a bunch of pampered weaklings, that's all.

Larissa's giving the lady another big smile, I can feel it. She shakes her hand, then watches her move away down the flagstone path, waiting for her to shut the garden gate before she turns to re-enter the house.

Her pupil's still banging away at his scales and arpeggios. Oh, he's got talent, no doubt about that. Hearing Lara close the door behind her, he breaks off and sits waiting in silence. Professor and pupil do not exchange a word. Lara settles into an armchair to the left of the boy and slightly behind him — the one she always uses for her lessons. She nods, and the redhead begins.

Chopin's *Etude N° 8*. My goodness! He certainly is taking it full tilt! You can tell he's been practicing all summer.

Lara always lets her pupils play their pieces straight through at the outset of the lesson, without any comments or interruptions. She even turns the pages for them, as if it were a concert perfor-mance. It's part of this absurd modern pedagogy. She says it's a mat-ter of respect; I call it indulgence. Don't see how it can possibly help to flatter these children. It's bad for them and it's bad for the music.

LARA

He's taking it much too fast.

So hard to convey to them that there's one right tempo and only one, a speed to be found and flowed with, and that all the other speeds are wrong.... In *The Man with the Camera*, Vertov runs through a series of stills — the face of an impoverished old woman vociferating against her fate, the face of a little girl astounded by a feat of magic — these are mere photographs, clichés, so to speak.... Then he begins stringing the images together and running them past us at the rate of twenty-four per second — and suddenly they become meaningful, they *make sense*, they seem to be life itself, truth and nature themselves; the faces quicken, they feel close and moving, and we empathize with them instantly. Although it's a silent film, you'd swear you can hear the old woman wailing in despair, the little girl crying out in astonishment.... Then Vertov again speeds up the stream of images — and the meaning vanishes. People go darting about like robots or machines, their movements are jerky and grotesque — they may look either laughable or monstrous but they're no longer human, their truth and humanity have disappeared....

It's the same thing with music. Of course the tempo's an artifice — but then, so's the piano itself, and Chopin's music, and art in general. Yet the eighty-eight half notes a minute which Chopin demands are *right*. As indisputably *right* as the twenty-four images a second.

Ah?.... Suddenly I stop listening. The notes, burning and ephemeral like fireworks, continue to soar through the air — for no one.

ALEXIS

At first I didn't notice anything unusual. But then I got to the middle of the right-hand page — I needed both my hands for playing, couldn't spare one even for an instant — and Madame Mestral didn't get up as she usually does to turn the page. I got a bit nervous because I'd soon be at the bottom of the page and I didn't know what came next, I hadn't learned the piece by heart, and if I stopped for even half a second the phrase would be mutilated, sliced in two — it would be a form of sacrilege, a crime against the music — so I started fidgeting on the bench and finally Madame Mestral came to her senses, leaping out of her armchair and turning the page just in the nick of time....

LARA

What happens next is Incredible. Impossible, and yet... An utter, silent surprise. A torrent. A warm gush, a shower of interiority, drenching my legs and the rug beneath me, splashing the piano pedals and my pupil's feet. A surprise — a total, blissful surprise. Warm for me, marvellous, yes — like sexual bliss, absolute and unexpected. Lasting only a few seconds. Incomprehensible. Never felt anything like it. Except perhaps — yes, decades ago — as a little girl, suddenly flooded with warmth in my bed, happy, amazed, until the acrid odour wafted up to my nostrils and the warmth turned into a clammy cold.... Alexis must have a similar association — still clinging desperately to the fabulous arpeggios of Chopin, he's blushed to his ears. His whole face has turned crimson. No, purple.

ALEXIS

Has Madame Mestral... has she...? No, it's too insane, it's unthinkable — nothing's happened at all....

LARA

And now, instead of the warm surprise, sharp pain. I freeze up, terrified. Distraught. Another miscarriage? Another dead baby? Oh God, oh my God, no, not that again, not this time, please....
"*Mamochka!*" I scream.

ALEXIS

It's too much. I can't take it. My hands are shaking, I have no idea what's going on, I wish I were somewhere else, I'm out of here, I'm already miles away. No. Still here. How do I get to my feet. How do I move. Don't even dare look at her, don't even want to guess what's going on. Never been in such an agony of indecision. Complete paralysis. My cheeks, scalp — my whole head in flames. Well, one way or another, something has to happen now....

I hear a door opening on the second floor. The sound of footsteps in the hallway, then on the stairs. Madame Mestral's mother. I've seen her before, wandering around the house like a ghost — a short, plump old lady, but light on her feet. Wrinkled and dumpy-looking, with piercing blue eyes. Hair pinned up in a straggly bun. Mother says she comes from Russia and speaks French with a heavy accent.

Perched on the edge of her armchair, Madame Mestral looks up pleadingly at her mother.... The old lady grasps the situation at once — yes, whatever it is I don't know, she knows. Giving a nod, she rushes over to the telephone, mutters something into the receiver — I can't make out what — and hangs up. Turns to me and stares straight at me with her laughing blue eyes. Very, very blue. Never seen eyes so blue.

"Go, my child," she says. "You can leave now. It is finished for today. Chopin will have to wait."

SOFIA

Chopin can wait. So can the roses and the delphiniums. This is a matter of life and death.

Oh, damn it — I expected as much — the buzzard next door has stuck his head out the window to spy on us. The old bugger! Now he'll rant and rave for days about the noise the ambulance is making. I wish he would croak! It's old folks like him that give old folks a bad name....

ROBERT

Look at her now, my lovely wife — a woman who's usually very civilized — clothed, shod, groomed, protected by a culture, an education, History, Europe, Western Civilization, and so forth, the piano.... Look at her now, lying nude and horizontal beneath a loose white smock, as the events occurring inside her body are projected onto screens in jagged lines and blinking lights — her most intimate physical processes, heart, blood, entrails, translating into electronic signals that mean *danger.*

Because. Because. Another being is striving to exist.

The vertical creatures are agitated and anxious. I, for instance, am vertical — I the maybe-father, maybe not, it all depends, plunged into turmoil, dragged out of a scientific conference at which I was to give a paper on the gregariousness of white mice.... Then there's Sofia, the maybe-grandmother — also vertical, albeit somewhat stooped. To say nothing of the nurses and doctors — vertical creatures all, thinking and sentient and singular — quite touching, really, each with his or her specific history, talents, penchants, neuroses — but at the moment no one gives a damn about all that; it's a matter of life and death. Pure, powerful emotion is held at bay by precise clinical words and gestures. Medical professionalism. Mastery.

White. Everywhere you look, all is white and sterile — the walls and ceilings, the sheets and coats, the masks, hats, gloves, slippers. Odd, when you think about it, how many of life's crucial experiences unfold against a white backdrop. Birth, death, madness.... the extremes, in which we cross the border between being and nothingness. Big words. Big things. Silence... screams... death rattles... tears. Before language, or beyond it. Invariably surrounded by the same, blank, suffocating whiteness.

"Fetal danger," Doctor Fabien is saying now.

"C-section," he says, two minutes later.

These are some of the words he pronounces. I glance at him, and our eyes meet above our white masks. Then I glance at my wife Lara, who can't quite decide which is worse — her own physical pain, or her fear for the child's life. The tug-of-war between the two must be wreaking havoc in her brain. She hates feeling so much at a loss, so helpless, so utterly at the mercy of others. Especially in front of her stoical mother. Fortunately, Sofia senses this and moves off. "I go sit in the hallway for a while," she tells the nurse. "My legs can't hold me up anymore. They're getting old." Crow's feet appear at the corners of the nurse's eyes — she must be smiling beneath her mask.

It all goes very fast. Suddenly Lara's no longer in pain. She's still there but her stomach isn't there anymore. I hold her hand, squeeze her hand, kiss her forehead, wipe her forehead, blow on her forehead — her abdominal muscles are being severed and it's of the utmost importance that we not be watching as this happens — so we gaze deeply into each other's eyes instead — I love you, Lara, do you realize, after all these years, Robert and Lara, Lara and Robert, and suddenly, silently, the myriad events of our lives converge, melding in this single gaze between us — yes, the ecstatic day of our first meeting, when I saw you at the opera, your back, your naked back at the piano, my love, I didn't hear a note you played, I couldn't take my eyes off your shoulder blades — and then, very gradually over the following months, I learned how fragile you were, the constant complaint just beneath the surface, that you didn't like yourself, that music didn't bring you happiness, and this made me want to love you all the more, for you *and* for myself — oh Lara, I remember how ravishing you were on our wedding day, I remember our trips abroad, all our breakfasts together, our quarrels and copulations.... And five years ago, the unexpected arrival of Sofia in our household, for health reasons.... And then — this great, miraculous hope at long last, after ten years of marriage and three miscarriages....

"What's her name?" asks Doctor Fabien, his voice at once serious and kind.

I look at you, Lara, and you look at me. We hadn't given the matter any thought. Neither boys' names nor girls' names. No names. Perhaps we'd felt it was still too soon, at five and a half months. Out of superstition — no names.

Our daughter has already left the room. We scarcely had time to catch a glimpse of her before the nurses rushed her off. Was that... it? Was that our... child, Lara? Good Lord... are you sure it wasn't... a sparrow...?

Doctor Fabien comes back into the room and says: "She weighs one pound eight ounces."

I hear him pronounce these words, and then some more words:

"We'll do everything in our power to save her... but you should be prepared."

He is extremely calm as he says this. He does not say it dramatically. His tone is almost cold, and for some reason I find this comforting. Words continue to issue from his lips.

"No prognosis as of yet," he says. "For the first seventy-two hours, everything is too precarious."

LARA

Live, my little one! Be strong! Live!

You're all but invisible in your glass bubble. A tiny fairy, trapped in a giant raindrop. I lean over, very close, to study you....

You've got a feeding tube inserted between your lips. I'm not allowed to nurse you yet — but I will — soon, you'll see — I'll give you all kinds of nourishment, earthly and celestial! For the time being, you're getting your food through an umbilical catheter. Icy, spider-shaped electrodes, taped to your chest, attentively follow your heartbeat. When the nurses approach your incubator, it's either to give you an injection in the heel or to palpate your scalp in search of an IV vein. The world is constantly aggressing you. Syringes and tubes, thermometers and needles keep entering you, puncturing your skin, probing your every orifice — and you cry. Soundlessly. Your face scrunches up in a perfect mimicry of weeping but you make no noise at all because your vocal chords are prevented from rubbing together by the ventilator tube passing between them....

Floating in a sort of limbo between this world and the next, you're connected to life by an incredibly flimsy thread — but I love you, my early bird. I love you and I'm going to save you! You'll see. I brought you into this world, and I won't let anyone take you out of it.

Live! O nameless one.

ROBERT

I drive home with Sofia, my mother-in-law. Glad to have her there next to me in the car, so solid, so utterly herself. Sofia will weather this crisis, no matter what its outcome. Her attitude is one of general and definitive resignation, but with a sense of humour. She's gone through worse than this. Much worse. Left her native Russia in the fifties, when her violinist husband Sergey brought her with him on a European tour. Walked out on him the minute they arrived in France, not knowing she was carrying his child at the time — *their* child, I mean, which then became *her* child — Lara, the woman I love.

"You know," says Sofia once we're in the kitchen, all the while pouring me a glass of Russian tea with a generous dollop of whisky in it, the way she knows I like it, the way she instinctively knows I need it right at the moment, feeling not so great just now, more than a little shaken by the sight of the sparrow that's supposed to be my child, our child, that bit of... whatever.... "In my country," she says, rolling her *r*'s in that inimitable way of hers, "they say the most vigorous grapevines are the ones planted in the soil with many stones. Yes. Because they must fight to put down roots. This makes them very strong. Don't worry! Your daughter will be strong, even stronger than the others. Not only she will live, she will go far. You will see."

I rather liked the grapevine metaphor....

Then she went over to the keyboard and started playing some little pieces — almost like children's dances — Tchaikovsky, maybe. She almost never plays the piano any more, but according to Lara she was a highly accomplished performer in her youth. Back in Moscow. Her little pieces cheer me up. I go on sipping my tea-and-whisky, and then I make myself a second one — this time without the tea.

At the hospital the next day, Lara reveals to me the name she's chosen for our daughter. It'll be Maya, she says. I don't answer. I mean, the main thing... what's the point of having a name, if....

And Doctor Fabien comes in to speak with us. As always, he simply states the facts, and I'm grateful for his firm, calm manner.

Lara's eyes shine brightly, I hold her by the hand, and the doctor's every word imprints itself upon our brains.

"The machines," he says.... "The machines can maintain your little girl in her current state, hovering between life and death. In a few days, Madame Mestral, you'll be able to go home — and then, as soon as you're up and about again, you'll come and visit her here. For the next few months, at least until she reaches term, you'll see her only here in intensive care, in a sterile milieu, hooked up to monitors. But throughout that period, your help is of the utmost importance. She needs to sense your breath of life in the depths of her being.... Only you, Madame Mestral, can give her the strength — the will to live... Only you can convince her not to let go."

Having pronounced these words, Doctor Fabien leaves the room. Lara and I stare at each other. Her eyes are shining even more brightly than before. No, no, not with tears. She isn't crying.

LARA

My early bird, my chickadee, my fledgling — o my minute, my all-but-invisible one, my palpitating pound and a half.... Look! Your ear is smaller than my thumbnail! A single one of my breasts is bigger than all of you! I contemplate you, work of art, work of artifice.

Nature is far away.... Flowers, trees, sunlight... nothing like that in here. There you lie, motionless in your box of steel and plexiglass — as spectacular as an aquarium or a theatre with its blue and white neon lights — a white mask over your eyes, tubes sprouting from your body, a red light blinking on your heel — oh my little extraterrestrial!

We're happy, aren't we? Yes! Happy!

I watch you, and you don't even notice, you're busy with more important things. Breathing, for instance. Snorting oxygen. This machine-mama comes down on you like an icy octopus, little one — grabbing your nostrils and noisily blowing air into your chest — it's because your lungs aren't formed yet, you haven't learned to breathe, so the machine has to do it for you....

Live! Maya my love.

ROBERT

I loved Lara more than ever, as I watched her affront the challenge of saving our daughter's life. My own working schedule kept me from visiting Maya during the week, but Lara went to see her every morning and stayed with her till dinner-time. Sitting next to the incubator, a sort of miniature ship made out of plexi-glass, she'd open the portholes and slip her hands inside, gently stroking our daughter and talking to her — talking — talking for hours on end. It pierced my heart. That whole time, my love for Lara was... almost overexposed; carried to a degree of incandes-cence that frightened me.

I couldn't live up to it... that's the way I see it now.

One Saturday afternoon, when I got to the hospital at around five, I saw that Lara was despondent, discouraged, tired beyond words. Our baby was inert. She'd only gained an ounce during the preceding week, her lungs still hadn't taken over from the machine — and she was far from being able to suck and swallow. We were finding it more and more difficult to believe that she might actu-ally leave the hospital some day, come home with us and sleep in the room we'd prepared for her.... The skin-on-skin sessions had been reduced to a few minutes a day, because Maya's temperature plunged the minute she left the incubator, so that instead of using her precious calories to put some flesh on her bones, she squan-dered them on heating up her body.... When I got there, the nurses had just covered her with a sheet of aluminum foil, so that the warmth emanating from her body would come back down on her instead of evaporating — like in one of those "Lo-Flame" cookers.

Lara turned to me, on the verge of tears, and said, "I can't take it anymore. I can't go on bearing the sole responsibility for her survival." (Oh yes, that lovely word *survival*. Our daughter will not only *re*vive, we told each other — she'll *sur*vive! I remember the day we invented that joke, and how good it felt to laugh at it together... and how painful it was, afterwards, remembering it....)

Anyway, Lara that day had clearly reached breaking-point. And I was the one who told her that she must hang on — that she mustn't let Maya hear her give in to despair.

As if Maya could hear anything, in the state she was in — about as big as your fist and as clenched as a fist. As if she had the

☾☽

slightest knowledge of her mother's moods! But that one sentence, which was basically an automatic response of encouragement on my part, acted on Lara like an electric shock. From then on, she clung to the notion that every word she said could affect, could influence the child....

Nothing was ever the same again.

LARA

My mother would send me to the far end of the house. You know, as far from the piano as possible. Then she'd play a note, and if I knew what it was, I could take a step forward. But if I got it wrong, I'd have to take a step back — can you *believe* that, Maya? Sometimes it took me a *whole hour* just to reach my mother at the piano. And all that just because I didn't have perfect pitch! But *your* pitch will be perfect, Maya. I'm sure of it. Look at your ear! It's absolutely perfect. So is your chin... and your nose. Yes, your nose is perfect, too — despite the tube that's blocking your nostrils just now, and running down your throat into your stomach!

I'll teach you myself at first — but gently, very gently, it's only a game, it's only happiness, I'll teach you everything I know and everything I don't know about music, the eighty-eight notes of the keyboard and the hundred million constellations in the sky — every note a star — including you, yes, a star, my little star — and you'll *play*, won't you? You'll know what it means to *play* — yes, like a child, like a game, the simplest, most natural thing in the world — yes, *you*, Maya, will be a true musician because — I can give you that, I've the power to give you anything in the world — life, music, laughter, joy, sunshine, rain.... *Look! Listen!*.... Yes, that's right, my little one, it's raining! That's right — and now the sun has come out. Tiny, iridescent droplets cling to the edges of the leaves and there, a huge rainbow inside each and every one.

ROBERT

A few days later, she came up with the idea of a story she could tell Maya — the story of her future life. She talked to her unceasingly about the piano, and about how she'd teach her music. She sat there all day, singing, humming, stroking her daughter's tiny body and talking to her... gradually convincing herself that our little Maya would become a phenomenal pianist.

Personally, it scared the shit out of me.

Lara, my Lara — unrecognizable. Obsessed... no, *possessed* by this mission she seemed to be on.

"Ordinarily," Doctor Fabien told me, drawing me aside, "your daughter would not have lived. Just ten years ago, a fetus born at twenty-four weeks instead of forty would have had no chance of survival."

And Lara: "This time, I'm going to win. This time, I'll do whatever needs to be done."

But we could have started over again, Lara! It wasn't too late; we could have tried to have a healthy, normal baby! Please, darling, I felt like telling her — let's create another child. What we're going through is just too painful. Oh, Lara please — wake up — come to your senses....

Whatever was going on, it was between the two of them — that much was clear. And I guess it was only natural. I did my best not to worry about it, telling myself it was just a phase — a very short phase, in the context of a lifetime — and that everything would soon be back to normal; I'd be at home, I'd have a wife on the one hand, a daughter on the other and a powerful connection to each.... But reason didn't help. I was disturbed by the strange symbiosis between them....

Sometimes, on my weekend visits, I myself would pick Maya up and press her to my chest. Her tiny body bristled with tubes and probes and drips — and her lack of weight made my head spin.

I don't know... the idea that I was holding an entire human being in my hands.... I could feel every bone in her body, every shudder that went through her, every one of her heartbeats — and I was afraid I'd break her, afraid she'd stop breathing in my hands. Her head was shaven because of the cranial IVs, her eyes were squeezed tightly shut, and... and, well, she wanted her mother, that much was clear.

Lara talked to her, all day, every day... and I felt she was losing herself in this endless flow of words — it was turning into a sort of delirium. At the hospital, she insisted on bathing and dressing Maya herself, and it was with great reluctance that she handed her over to the nurses for shots and tests. At home, she almost never slept — and even when she did, I could have sworn she continued talking to Maya in her sleep.

It made me nervous. I'm a man of science. I need to have firm ground beneath my feet, that's just the way I am. Whatever was happening was at odds with everything I believed in. With the character I'd forged for myself. With my values, my outlook on life. I admit it.

MONSIEUR RAQUET

Oh for Chrissake, now she's brought her goddamn brat home with her. I thought he'd croaked, and good riddance. Hadn't heard the piano since the day of the ambulance, so I thought the kid was stillborn and the mother off someplace, blubbering in a corner. Peace at last! I said to myself. But no, now she's brought the brat home, goddammit. And I can look forward to days and days filled with screeching and wailing. Can't get a minute of rest, in this so-called peaceful neighbourhood. Until the day I die, I'll just be going back and forth between two forms of torture — the goddamn piano and the goddamn yowler.

LARA

Your father is going to leave us, Maya.

Robert will leave me. Not for another woman — no, nothing like that — but he'll distance himself little by little, and end up moving out for good. So you'll grow up without a father, just as I did. We repeat the very things we had sworn never to repeat. We inflict on our children the pain we ourselves endured... how can we do otherwise?

After the divorce, it'll be just the two of us.... No, the three of us, counting Babushka.... Yes, there'll be three females in the household — and three pianos!

ROBERT

I left.

Not right away, no. It took me almost two years to get up the courage to leave — but my departure started back then, shortly after Maya came home from the hospital.

I still love them, though. Both of them. My wife; my daughter. I love them passionately, and I can't live with them. That's the way it is.

It's so strange, when you think about it. I had everything, and God knows I cared about what I had. The beautiful big house with the garden and the pianos. The woman I loved, the love of my life....

Maybe sometimes... people don't really want to have everything. Sometimes they reject what they love, just so they won't have everything. I don't know how else to explain it.

LARA

You know, Maya, when you were young, Maya, Maya, when you were just a little girl, I mean when I was just a little girl, you know, even littler, I'd go hide under the piano while my mother was playing, the piano would be like my house, my log cabin — and Mamochka would play and play — and everything around me would be humming and vibrating with sound, *boom*, the low notes, the pedal — a storm, a flood, a hurricane of music raging through the woods, millions of notes raining down out of the sky, brilliant flashes of lightning in the high notes, and then *boom* again — and I LOVED IT!

You'll sit under the piano, too, won't you? And later on, whenever you're ready, you'll sit down at the keyboard. Naturally, you'll have to get used to the complaints of our neighbour, Monsieur Raquet.... He's a bitter man — his wife died ages ago and his children never come to visit, he hates life, so of course he hates music, too, and on the evenings when the ensemble comes over to practise he calls the police and tells them we're "disturbing the peace" — isn't that incredible? "Disturbing the peace" with Brahms's *Trios* at seven o'clock in the evening? Anyway, the old geezer will eventually leave this world, and the three of us will throw a big party to celebrate. Yeah... for once we'll *really* disturb the peace, won't we? Then some new neighbours will move in next door.... Lovely people... an artist in his fifties... yes, Lucien... and his adolescent son... no, his nephew....

MAYA

A mover's truck! Parked almost right in front of our house!

SOFIA

Maya leaps to her feet and dashes outside — I can see her from up here at my bedroom window. She looks even younger than ten, more like a fairy than a human girl. Lara's worried about her hair — short black wisps of it, sticking up all over her head, as if she'd just received an electric shock — it's because they shaved her skull when she was born, the doctor says it might stay like that forever — well, no matter, I find my Vnouchka lovely just the way she is. Quivering and waif-like, her summer dress clinging to her body.

Lara follows her out of doors, dressed with a French sort of elegance: tailored suit, handbag, chignon. It's nearly time to leave for the audition. I can tell she's jittery from the way she crushes her handbag to her side. How dare she be jittery? How can she have even an instant of doubt...?

LUCIEN

Getting too old to move house. I can feel it. Wish I couldn't. Turns out there actually is such a thing as youth — ha! — who would have believed it? Back in the good old days, Annette and I used to love moving house. It showed how strong and impetuous and efficacious we were, in spite of our intellectual professions. Ah, it was great! We'd summon our muscles and they'd stand to attention. We'd rejoice in feeling the strain in our limbs and backs. We'd pant and sweat and grumble and have a ball. Proud of doing the whole thing by ourselves — lugging boxes, building book-shelves, renting pick-up trucks... all over now. So many things are over. Including Annette herself — and repeating this to myself when I wake up every morning doesn't keep me from forgetting it again and again through the day, and all night long. Ah, the pan-creas... yes, that's one of the worst... that's a ruthless, relentless... Fed up to the teeth with hearing it. Whence this move. Yes. Need to live in a part of the city where no one ever knew Annette. Or me with her.

SOFIA

Grunting and grimacing with the effort, the musclemen lower an upright piano down from the back of the truck. Maya claps her hands and jumps for joy. As if our three pianos weren't enough! But of course they aren't. To a real musician, every instrument is a new encounter, a revelation. The musclemen turn around and plunge back into the yawning maw of the truck; the owners of the piano must be in the house — there's no one in sight.

No one anywhere in the world. Only the little one and her instrument.

She undoes the canvas cover with flying fingers, pulls it up and pushes it back — just far enough to be able to open the piano lid, laying bare the keyboard. That's all she needs. A keyboard, a universe. And she starts to play. Just like that, sitting on an upended cardboard box. Child's play. Bach's *Prelude in E minor*. The musclemen keep going back and forth, head down, as if nothing were happening. Bunch of *lumpen!* Boeotians! Beasts! But the new owner — a man in his fifties with longish white hair — ah, at least *he's* got ears! He emerges from the house with his adolescent son and both of them just stand there, transfixed. No women in the vicinity. I wish they had a huge family — a clan. I wish the whole neighbourhood would crowd around to listen! That's how it used to be in Moscow, whenever there was a real concert, a genius. Gould, for instance, played the first part of his concert before fifty people, they begged him to extend the intermission another half an hour — and when he came back on stage there were two thousand people in the audience! Word of mouth. Back then, people knew what mattered. A great pianist is an emergency.

They don't understand that sort of thing anymore these days, with their canned music. Still... look at these guys, dear Lord ! Yes, both the father and the son are flabbergasted by my little elf, aren't they? Sitting right there on the sidewalk, making that rickety upright produce sounds it didn't know it had in it! Ha! Listen to that, will you? That's my Vnouchka for you! That little girl plays the way people used to walk, with her feet on the ground and her eyes on the starry heavens. I'm so proud of her!

Thank You, God. On my knees I'd thank You, if I could still get down on my knees.

LUCIEN

She was just my age. Fifty-five. When people say, "Goodness! So young!" they can't quite make it sound convincing. Fifty-five really isn't young — but it's not really old, either. It's an age, unlike twenty or twenty-five, when most people would seriously prefer not to die.

But you've got to get a grip on yourself — it's a social obligation. You're allowed twelve months of mourning, not a minute more. No overtime. When your year's up, you're expected to stop waving the photo of your wife in everybody's face... stop telling the whole story... put it behind you.

Yeah. So... you tell the university you've decided to retire. Early retirement, as the saying goes. Not that early at all, if the truth be told. Mm-hm. That's right; you need a change of pace, of neighbourhood, of air....

First time since May '68 that I've moved alone. And with professional help.

And also the help of Benjamin, my insect-crazy nephew. Kids are not my cup of tea, generally speaking — Annette and I saw eye-to-eye on that, which explains how we remained lovers for three decades. Still, I'm pretty fond of Benjamin. He's not a bullshit artist, like most kids his age. At fourteen, he's got his own world, that's what I like about him. It may be structured by beetles and roaches and spiders, but at least it's structured. He asks questions, does experiments, records and double-checks the results... in silence....

I'm glad to take a load off my brother's shoulders by looking after Benjamin this summer. He and his wife have got *six* youngsters, poor things. Another victory for John Paul II....

Who knows? Maybe in his dreams, Benjamin carries out his experiments on his swarm of younger siblings....

BENJAMIN

Like a dragonfly — alighting, just barely alighting — what on earth *is* this apparition, this blue-green iridescent girlchild.... Her fingers flutter to and fro, gathering beauty wherever they find it and finding it everywhere. Unbelievable. Usually I could care less about classical music. But *this* — such elation, such exhilaration — I mean, look. And she's laughing, too — laughing and playing at the same time — as if the music were tickling her from head to toe. And meanwhile, Uncle Lucien — a statue. A frowning statue. He's enjoying it, that much is clear — and not just with his eardrums.

He's changed since Auntie Annette died; he's gotten sort of old-fogyish. I only hope he doesn't bring out that photo of her in Merida. "This is my wife... well, this *was* my wife.... Isn't she... er... wasn't she beautiful?" Bugs the hell out of me when he does that. Always watching for people's eyes to light up — "Oh, my! Yes, just beautiful!" — what else can they say?

I mean, a little self-control....

LUCIEN

So beautiful.... We'd spent three months together in Mexico that winter, thinking it was a winter like any other, never imagining it might be the last.... Annette is absolutely smashing in that photo. Half-reclining amidst red and gold cushions on a bench...

dressed in baggy orange silk pants... a little halter top setting off her lovely tanned arms... narrow-strapped leather sandals... a long saffron-coloured scarf draped around her neck with a grace and nonchalance which were hers alone... she's staring straight into the camera lens and smiling at me... a real smile, at once trusting and mischievous.... God, how her smiles used to keep me warm! Shortly after her death, I had two hundred copies of the photo made and passed them out to everyone — friends, acquaintances, even chance encounters.... The idea that dozens of people all over the world would be carrying *this* image of Annette in their minds — a warm and luminous Annette, smiling, surrounded by red and yellow, orange and saffron.... helped me blot out the unbearable memories. Annette transformed into an Auschwitz survivor. Abject. Eaten away by illness. Gnawed to the bone. Vomiting, weeping, defecating. Annette's smooth soft flesh rotting, melting away before my eyes, Annette pleading with the pain to have done with her quickly, as quickly as possible — if possible, more quickly still.

No, my love. I won't show your photo around anymore. I want to spend the time that's left to me on this planet making stained-glass windows, in an attempt to recapture something of the light in your eyes....

MAYA

Never played on such a tinny old piano in my life! Bach — on the scrap heap! What a riot!

BENJAMIN

Ah — it's over now. The little one jumps up, spins around and takes a bow, electric hair, mosquito body, legs everywhere, walking ravening burrowing jumping swimming, not faking shyness like other girls her age, not putting on airs, eyes still lit up from the music, she looks straight at us and says, "Hi! We live next door" — raising a slender arm to show us where — "My name's Maya. Is this your piano?"

No no, not at all, it just happened to turn up amidst the rest of our belongings. Then — as the movers go on dragging and shoving and lugging Uncle Lucien's junk into the house — everyone launches into introductions. First names only, the ice already being broken. Lara the mother, very *grande dame*, frozen smile, how are you, so pleased to meet you, shaking hands around the circle, Uncle Lucien makes me laugh by presenting himself as a painter on glass, oh I don't blame him, it's only natural he should want to be someone else, he and Auntie Annette were professors and nomads but now that she's gone on to a better world he needs a place to hide — and what better place than in this ritzy-shitsy neighbourhood? "I hope you'll drop by some-day, once I've got my workshop set up," he tells the dragonfly. "It'd be a pleasure to have you." I glance around to see if my box of silkworms has come out of the truck by any chance — nope, no such luck, no sign of it yet. "I noticed there was a hole in the fence between our houses," Uncle Lucien is saying now to the uptight lady, "right behind the apple tree. Benjamin and I would be happy to fix it. We can do it tomorrow morning if you'd like!" "Oh, that hole doesn't bother me," says the woman, staring at Lucien with an odd look on her face, as if she were thinking about something else. Then she adds, "On the con-trary — it's quite convenient! That way Maya can visit you without having to go out to the street. And... and you'll come and see us, too, won't you? It'll be our secret passageway." I must be dreaming, they just met three minutes ago and they're already talking secret passage-ways? Boy, she doesn't waste any time! Must be Lucien's great sad eyes that have gone to her head....

Just then, a flamboyant red Alfa Romeo thunders up; screeches to a halt right behind the moving truck. "Daddy!" cries the mosquito

— and a guy gets out, suit-and-tie sort of guy, with a face to match his car, same general look I mean — which is not surprising, since he's the one who chose his car — chose his face, too, in a way — all bright and shiny, just the opposite of my uncle who's always a bit unkempt, disheveled, bearish — looks like a nice guy, though, the daddy I mean, the man that just drove up, he flashes a smile full of white teeth at us and plants a big kiss on the nape of the grasshopper's neck — she's got her legs wrapped around his waist now, skinny spiderlegs — then he sets her down, kisses his wife, greets the rest of us, more hand-pumping all around the circle, Robert his name is — and right away, Lucien puts his foot in it. "I'm your new neighbour," is all he says, but it turns out to be a gaffe, the guy corrects him, laid-back, no hassle: "Well," he says, "welcome to the neighbourhood. I myself don't live here anymore, though. I just come on the weekends."

In that case, it's weird how he kissed his wife — his ex-wife, rather — a tender smoochy sort of kiss, not the chilly brushing of cheeks you generally get between divorcees, anyway, whatever, no skin off my back, who cares how they kiss, all I care about are my silkworms, where the hell are they, hope they haven't been crushed beneath the sixty boxes of Uncle Lucien's books. "Your daughter's quite a musician," he says now, to change the subject, make up for his earlier blunder, land on *terra ferma* by saying something irrefutable this time — and the mother gasps, "Oh my goodness, we really must run — Maya has an audition downtown in twenty minutes" — so at last the little group disperses, bye-bye, bzzz-bzzz, like so many bees, each zooming off in search of what it thinks of as nectar.

ROBERT

Well, at least these neighbours will be a change from that dreadful Monsieur Raquet.... Between the stained-glass windows and the earthworms, looks like there's a fascinating summer ahead....

I stand on the front steps watching Lara and Maya as they move off down the street — one tall and the other small; one solemn and the other spirited. Looking at them, you'd swear it was Lara who was preparing for an ordeal. Her step is stiff, tragic, almost petrified — whereas Maya, even as she holds her mother's hand, is hopping and skipping about like a will-o'-the-wisp — the audition is clearly the last thing on her mind....

Poor Lara. She's always had stage fright. Used to describe it to me in great detail after every concert... First she'd get a sudden rush of adrenalin, then the blood would stop circulating in her hands and feet, she'd start to tremble, her fingers would turn to ice, her mind would go blank, the score would be unrecognizable — *"What are all these notes for?"* — and she'd be convinced of her impending failure... though I could never grasp exactly what this "failure" might entail — she could only describe it to me with the help of metaphors, images of walls and waves, collisions and drowning. Being a practical sort of person, I would suggest she take Inderal. Almost all stage performers use it and it works like a charm, preventing the release of adrenalin so they remain in full possession of their powers.... Lara takes pills almost every night for her insomnia — why not for her stage fright? She did try Inderal once — but she got the dosage wrong, took eighty milligrams instead of five, and it calmed her down so much she didn't even feel like putting her hands to the keyboard....

Where does Schumann fit into all this? Well, Schumann spent long years wrestling with the same ghosts... important not to forget that.

When I finally go into the house, Sofia's waiting for me at the kitchen table. She lived for so many years in Moscow community apartments, she still thinks everything important happens in the kitchen. She serves me my usual comforting concoction, tea and whisky. Weird... it's been eight years since the divorce, and I feel still more comfortable here than in the apartment I share with

Nathalie in another city. Instantly at ease. I keep an old pair of slippers in the upstairs bedroom, a toothbrush in the bathroom... and every once in a while... Lara lets me come to her as before. Nathalie probably guesses as much, but she prefers not to ask questions. She'd rather tell herself I'm a doting daddy who stays with his gifted little girl on weekends because she can't do without her pianos for so much as a day.... Still, I'm sure that some part of her brain is aware... that Lara and I....

Lara's is the only body that can truly move me — the body that miraculously opened up, one day ten years ago, and brought forth Maya. All week long the pain of our separation torments me, and on the weekend — the minute I get here and take Lara and Maya in my arms — it vanishes. I love them... but somehow what I love now is Lara-and-Maya in one word, the two of them together, in that mysterious symbiosis of the white room that always excluded me. It's as if this house were filled with the light of a fierce sun — whereas, my eyes being what they are, I can only bear electric lighting. Deep down, our divorce hasn't changed a thing — Lara will always be my wife and Sofia my mother-in-law, but in my day-to-day life I need to be with someone who's easy-going and efficient, not high-strung... someone like Nathalie.

"And your Natalia is doing well?" asks Sofia, who cannot seriously conceive of a woman's name ending with a letter other than *a*.

"Yes, she's fine, thanks."

The range of meanings that can be covered by a little phrase like "Fine, thanks" is extraordinary. No reason for me to bore Sofia with a blow-by-blow account of Nathalie's hassles at the medical journal. You ask a polite question, you get a polite answer and *alles in Ordnung*. Courtesy is one of the most brilliant inventions of the human race. I've always enjoyed listening to Algerian women when they run into each other in the street — their salaams are empty of semantic content but full of so many other things. "And your health is fine?" "And your son is fine?" "And your husband is fine?"

"And your mother is fine?" "And your grandsons are fine?" "And your daughters are fine?" "Good then, good, everything is fine." An admirable convention.

However, after a few minutes of this reassuringly banal exchange, I ask Sofia a real question: "And how's Lara doing?"

"So-and-so," she answers.

Her command of English may be shaky, but it doesn't keep her from getting her meaning across.

"She's got insomnia?"

"Yes, I think."

"What about you? How's that high blood pressure of yours?"

"That's between me and the good Lord," Sofia retorts with the brusquerie I love — her way of showing affection. "You want to worry, go worry about your mice."

LARA

Yes, I'll take care of your training myself at first — but later on, when you get to be ten or twelve and I have nothing left to teach you, you'll have an audition with the great Dianescu — yes my little angel, yes my early bird — nothing but the best for you, if only you'll consent to stay alive. We'll walk to the audition together, hand in hand, and you'll be gay and carefree won't you darling — because I will have given you the gift of all gifts, music as a game — yes, you'll have the *gift* of music my love, everything your fingers touch will turn into joy — listening to you, Dianescu will fall over backwards in astonishment!

Of course you won't be the first prodigy he's ever seen. He thinks he knows what prodigies are — prodigies are children with sadistic parents. He's seen armies of them, the poor things, obliged to play their instrument three, then four, then five, six, seven hours a day, and threatened with missing supper or even being whipped if they don't, children whose mothers bring them sponge balls the minute they take their hands off the keyboard because they mustn't waste a second, they can keep their finger muscles active by kneading the ball — "Careful, now! Don't flatten out those knuckles! Keep those fingertips rounded!" Yes, all the pitiful, piteous prodigies, locked up with their pianos and sentenced to forced labour upon them, condemned to produce beauty, required to shine and excel to compensate for the many disappointments and failures of their parents — oh yes, he's seen more of these so-called virtuosos than he cares to remember — cut off from all contact with their peers, taken out of school, deprived of games, sports, hikes, trips of all kinds, as these activities entail risks for their ten priceless appendages... but in your case, Maya, it won't happen that way.

You will *live* in music — it will be your natural environment — playing will come as easily to you as breathing — oh, *breathe, my little one! breathe, I beseech you!* Listening to you, Dianescu will have none of the silly, conventional reactions you see in films about prodigies — mouth dropping open, eyebrows shooting up — no, he'll just grow slightly more still, his gaze will become serious and attentive and I'll know that the answer is yes. Yes — he'll take you in hand and guide your steps from here on in, helping you come closer, ever closer to your true home, the sublime place that was your starting point in life....

Oh — if only you will live!

DIANESCU

I can't bear their hope any longer.

Must be a lot like what cancerologists endure. Hope — imploring, urgent, terrible hope in the eyes of every patient. Please, doctor! Please pronounce the magic word. I know you have hundreds of terminally ill patients, but tell me that *for me* — *me*, you understand, the human soul you can see burning in my eyes here and now, beseeching you — for *me* it's different. Tell me, oh, tell me I'll be the exception. The survivor. The genius.

I've had it. Can't put up with them anymore. I'm getting mean, I know. The more they waste my time, the meaner I get. The young girl this morning, for instance. Flew all the way from San Francisco just to get my opinion, my advice, a word of encouragement. Didn't look like she was rolling in it, either — plane ticket must have swallowed her family's savings. A Chicano, I think they call them over there. Mexican origins, not bad-looking if you like the Hispanic type, long ebony hair, olive complexion, big dark imploring eyes, here we go again, I've had it. These kids have gotten too much applause. The minute they show the slightest sign of talent, they get flowers heaped on them, recitals, prizes, conservatories, it puffs up their egos and fills their brains with silly illusions. So... well, maybe I *did* go a bit far with the Chicana. She paid for the others, let's put it that way... and it won't kill her. I couldn't help it, she was wasting my time and suddenly I saw red. She sat down at the keyboard, looked up at me shyly, and told me she'd spent the whole spring putting this audition together. Who gives a damn? Then she began. Okay, Scriabin, Debussy, Messiaien, why not.... I could see her gradually relaxing, forgetting her stage fright and starting to *express* herself — conveying what her teacher had no doubt taught her was *emotion*. To me, her technique was an open book, and a lousy book at that, some sort of Harlequin romance, now you're supposed to weep, now you're frolicking in the flowers, ah, and now, look at the beating of the fairy wings! Suddenly I couldn't take it anymore... all these talented brats who think they're world caliber already — so I cut her off.

That's right. I cut her off. Just like that. "Tell me, my dear Esmeralda," I said — I think that's what her name was — "do you know how to sing?"

A bit taken aback, of course.

"Yes? I'm sure you have a lovely voice. Do sing something for me."

Hesitating and blushing, she began to play and sing one of Benjamin Britten's *Michelangelo Sonnets*. Her voice was thin and tremulous — she had no idea what I was getting at. Not yet. She'd soon find out.

"No, no... excuse me," I said, cutting her off again. "Just — *sing*, if you'd be so kind. *Without* the piano."

She held out for another couple of bars, then fell silent. Eyes on the floor, cheeks burning. Rather attractive, a blush on dark skin. Then I let her have it. "Listen, my dear Esmeralda," I told her in my most cynical, world-weary voice. "Do me a favour. Go home to San Francisco. Sing, if you feel like it. Dance! You're not bad-looking, you could be an actress, a model, a call-girl, whatever you like! But I beseech you, *please stop playing the piano*."

Ha! She was out of there fast. Good riddance. I can't be bothered with the mood swings of every pseudo-artist in the world. This time I've made up my mind: as of next year I'll stop taking on new students. What's the point of teaching, anyway? In thirty years of piano pedagogy, I've only encountered two or three pianists.

And this one now. Here we go again. The elf child — I'm familiar with that variety as well. *Wunderkind*, my eye. Got it: one glance at the mother and the situation is clear, the anxiously knit brow, the circles under her eyes, an insomniac, a druggy, ten to one she took advantage of the shadows in the cloakroom to gulp down some Xanax, probably a failed pianist herself, let's see what sort of spiel she's cooked up for the occasion.... "Good afternoon, Monsieur Dianescu, it's truly an honour to shake your hand." Oh Christ, I expected as much. Glenn Gould was right, you should never shake peoples' hands, it's degrading.... "Your friend Monsieur Taittinger suggested I take advantage of your presence in the city.... Otherwise I'd never have presumed...." All right, make it short, so many words for nothing, so many seconds soaring past us one after the other and biting the dust, get to the point…. "I myself teach piano at the Conservatory, and I've handled Maya's training up until now, but…." Fine, I know what comes next, let's go on to the keyboard. "Madame," I break in abruptly, "we have two ears and one tongue, to invite us to speak less and listen more. I've always found this saying of Plutarch's very relevant. Do begin."

Ah?

LARA

You'll play a Bach *Fantasy*, except that it will be as if you'd composed it yourself — no, as if you were a bird and this *Fantasy* were your song. Listening to you, Dianescu and I will grow more and more serene with every passing instant — because it's no longer even a question of notes, mistakes, fingerings or technique — your hands run across the keyboard just as your feet might run across a sandy beach — because you *want* to and you *can* run. Yes, as your tiny fingers go on striking and stroking the black and white keys, we gradually sink into a state of bliss. Oh, my angel — you dominate — yes, look, you conquer the instrument that's always conquered me — it's your *instrument*, in other words, totally at your service. The eight-hundred-pound black monster arches its back, rubs up against you and lets you pet it like a cat.

Seeing the absolute immobility of Dianescu's stare and the slightly irritated tapping of his right hand on the piano top, I know exactly what he'll say when you stop playing: "First lesson in Berlin, mid-September. Here's the address." Ah, my little early bird! You're learning to fly with your own wings! Soon you won't need me any more….

But what's worse is that music won't need me any more either.

MAYA

Look, Mama, it's raining! Ohhh! Remember how heavy and clammy the air was this afternoon? Remember how the big fat moving men were pouring with sweat as they carried the boxes? The storm must have come to a head while we were at the audition — we missed the thunder and lightning but now the whole world is being washed clean — isn't it *wonderful?* Come on, let's hold hands and run! Aren't you *happy*, Mama? "Yes — very." You say yes very, but you look sad. What are you sad about, Mama? It went well, didn't it? That piano was fantastic, the two of us hit it off right away! I'll be taking lessons from that man, going to Germany twice a month — let's celebrate! Look, there's a bakery — will you buy me some chocolate meringues? Thank-you, Mama! I just *love* meringues, I could eat *fifty* of them, running with you in the rain! And we don't even have to be careful, we can eat like pigs and the rain will wash the chocolate off our faces! Mmm, they're *delicious...* want another one? All right, I'll stop stuffing my face, I didn't know we had to save some for dessert.

Look how the leaves dance when the raindrops hit them! All the trees are just jiggling for joy! You're really beautiful with your hair wet, Mama — and I love holding hands with you when we go out walking together, and seeing our fingers all woven together like a basket — do you think my fingers will be as long as yours when I grow up? Do you think I'll be able to play an octave and two notes the way you do?

Look how happy your roses are — they're just gulping down the rain, chug-a-chug, you won't need to water them tonight.... Hey! Did you see that? There's a bunch of little *froggies* in our garden! They must've come out to celebrate the rain, too! That was neat when you said the hole in the fence would be our secret passage... Our new neighbors seem really nice, don't they? — Hey! What was that, a *fox* ? Did you see it? Over there.... It's gone.... I swear it looked just like a fox! Maybe it lives in the forest and it got lost.... Can foxes get lost, Mama?

SOFIA

Goodness, my daughter is absent-minded this evening — she hasn't even noticed that Maya's hair is dripping wet. How can she let her sit down at the table with rain still running down her neck? Come over here, you, let me rub your head with the towel — there you go. Now sit down and enjoy your meal. I made stuffed cabbage especially for you — go ahead, eat! You deserve to eat well, after what you did this afternoon. Oh, not that I had the slightest doubt as to the outcome — I knew it would be yes. A gift from God isn't something you hem and haw about. You don't say, well, maybe, I'll have to see, it depends on my schedule.... It's *yes*, and there's an end to it — nothing more to be said.

The little one doesn't care a bit! All she cares about is that her mama's bought her a bagful of meringues and her papa's here, the family's together. Bach or meringues, either's fine with her. It's bizarre, at her age, such a strong taste for counterpoint. Never heard of such a thing. At the Conservatory in Moscow, we all considered Bach as good finger exercise, not real music. All of us were dripping with romanticism — Liszt, Schumann, Beethoven, virtually nothing before Mozart. But ever since she discovered the *Little Anna Magdalena Bach Book* at age four, Maya's had an overriding passion for those stiff, archaic forms — fugues, chaconnes, passacaglias.... It's really very unusual.

"So how do you like my stuffed cabbage?"

"What stuffed cabbage?"

"Okay, so you liked it."

Larissa seems preoccupied this evening. She keeps drumming her fingers on the edge of the table, as if to keep them limber....

What *is* the matter with her? Maya did well at her audition, she was dazzling, Dianescu had no choice but to take her — wasn't that what she wanted? Oh, French women are so complicated. You ask them a question, and instead of answering they start talking about ambivalence, love-hate... all that Freudian claptrap. Well, that's what happens when you don't let the good Lord show you the way — you feel responsible for every step you take, and the slightest choice becomes an agony....

I talked to Him about this whole audition thing. He told me Dianescu was an excellent idea, and then He arranged things so it would all come off. Simple as pie — and I'm delighted. Why does Lara have to complicate things? Must be the genes of Seriojka, her melancholy father.... Well, nothing I can do about it.

"Papa, what would you do if the white mice got out of their cages and started running all over the laboratory? How would you catch them?"

"Uh... wait a minute, let me think.... Well, I'd ask the cheese-maker to make me an enormous cat out of Swiss cheese. That way the mice would come up close, attracted by the smell — but then, torn between fear and greed, daring neither to come closer nor to back off, they'd be glued to the spot, and I'd take advantage of their indecision to throw a giant net over them!"

Maya bursts out laughing and so do I, but Larissa goes on staring into the void. She hasn't heard a word since the beginning of the meal — I wonder where she is.

Odd, very odd.

"Come on, Maya," I say, getting to my feet. "Time for bed. Call me when you're ready, all right?" And I begin to clear the table.

"Don't bother with that, Sofia," says Robert. "You've spent the afternoon slaving over a hot stove. Lara and I will do the washing-up, it'll be a pleasure."

"Oh!" I cry indignantly. "Put that plate down and go smoke your pipe and read your newspaper in the drawing-room like a man!

Aren't you ashamed of yourself, sticking your nose into women's business?"

Ah, this new fashion they've got in Europe! Unisex, they call it. Ridiculous. Men putting on aprons and doing dishes, or carrying their babies around in bags on their stomachs, I never saw anything so preposterous in my life! If the good Lord had wanted men to carry babies around, He would have given them a womb. Period. It's obvious.

"Larissa, wake up, you're in the clouds!"

"Yes, Mamochka...."

She smiles at me. I know that smile. It means she's suffering. *Can't you see that today marks a tragic turning-point?* she's saying to herself. Yes, I can read my daughter's mind. *From now on*, she's thinking, *Maya will begin to move away from us.... She'll have a brilliant career....*

Don't worry, Lara. What's the point in torturing yourself? Let the good Lord take care of that. Meanwhile, I'm going up to put the little one to bed.

Every night while I'm sleeping, a carpenter comes to change the staircase. When I wake up in the morning, each stair has been raised by half an inch. Before long I won't be able to climb these confounded stairs anymore. Take it easy, my precious heart. Take it easy... don't beat so fast! You've only got so many beats left, and you mustn't squander them! I want to see what becomes of my little musician.... Give me a little more time... just a little more....

LARA

Babushka will worship you, Maya. You'll fulfill all the dreams she had for me. Her daughter may have disappointed her, but her Vnouchenka will more than make up for it....

And yet... in a way... *you are me*, aren't you, darling?... since I'm the one who made you, brought you to life by stroking you with my hands and voice, talking to you, day after day... so how could your happiness make me anything but happy? When you breathe in, my lungs fill up with air; when you laugh, my heart jumps for joy. Oh, I know... you're not really up to laughing yet... but sometimes, now, when they take the feeding tube out of your throat, a little smile plays on your lips. Your eyes are tightly shut, so you must be smiling at angels.... I'm fighting to bring you down to earth, Maya, but you'll always have a precise and intimate remembrance of this time when you lived so close to heaven.... Whence your passion for Bach, Gesualdo, Gibbons... all the composers who, like yourself, were once touched by the gods.

Isn't it luscious in here? Tucked away together in the white room, curled up in our bubble of warmth in the depths of an icy winter, a space outside of space, the minutes swelling and flowing around us, a time outside of time, I press you to me in the rocking-chair, your skin melts into mine, my body teaches yours the regular back-and-forth movements of rocking, I feel so calm, I love you so intensely my little one, I never dreamed such a love was possible — and now, when you open your eyes, you actually *look* at me! A sharp thrill goes through me every time — *oh, you're there!* Don't worry, Maya, we'll come through this together, I promise you.

Every evening after supper, Babushka will go up to your room so that you can play her something on the piano — and afterwards, she'll tell you a story to go with what you've just played. I'll hear you from afar as I do the washing-up downstairs... first the piano, then the voices.

Where did my mother get the idea for this lovely ritual? She never used it with me. Nothing but *la, do, fa* — and the steps I was allowed to take — now forward, now back.

SOFIA

Phew! At last, the armchair! Thank you, dear Lord, for inventing armchairs; that was extraordinarily kind of You.

"Wait a minute, Maya! Wait — I have to catch my breath or I won't hear a single note you play. There, that's better now.... Go ahead."

I'm eager to hear her. She always finds something to surprise me. Either the phrasing, or the *staccati*, or a particular use of the pedal.... Tonight, it's the slow tempo. The C-minor fugue from the *Well-Tempered Harpsichord*.... I close my eyes and ease myself gently into the music like a warm bath. Yes. Yes, my Vnouchenka, *that's it*. Her silences reach out to one another from between the crystalline notes.

Ah! And then she launches into a brilliant, technically daunting prelude, sloughing over the difficulties by taking it much too fast — and I protest. "Humph! Speed!" I tell her. "You think you can impress me with your speed? At that rate, music goes nowhere — fast!"

And, as always when I berate her, Maya bursts into laughter and throws her arms around my neck.

LARA

Afterwards, you'll carefully close the piano lid and crawl into bed. And there, as your body gradually adjusts to the night, you'll await your Babushka's story with open eyes.... That evening, since you played to her so frenetically, Sofia decides to tell you a story in which music serves as a punishment — the story of Ivan and his magic violin.

SOFIA

Young Ivan hires himself out to Master Penny-Pincher. He works for a whole year, and at the end of the year his master dismisses him with no other wages than a bit of bacon and a chunk of bread. But Ivan is a gay-hearted man, so he sets out joyfully with a song on his lips. Just as he's crossing a little bridge over the river, he runs into an old man. "Good day to you, young lad!" says the man "You seem in excellent spirits, all is well with you, but the same cannot be said of everyone. I myself am starving — you wouldn't have a little something to share with me, would you?" Ivan has very little — but still, he feels that he should share it. So he says, "Gladly, father!" and the two men sit down together and eat the bread and bacon. Just as he is leaving, the old man says to Ivan, "Since you were generous with me, I'll be generous with you. You can ask me for whatever you want, and your wish will be granted." Ivan says, "I'd love to have a violin that would make people dance when I play it." The old man answers him with a smile, "That violin's already in your pouch! And I've tossed in a few other goodies, too." And before he's finished speaking, the old man vanishes into thin air.

"Hm!" says Ivan to himself. "That cannot have been an ordinary passer-by."

Opening his pouch, he discovers a beautiful violin. And next to the violin, a roast chicken hot off the spit, a bottle of wine, and a purse full of gold coins! Ivan, delighted, sits down to a second meal, polishes off the chicken and begins to count his gold. Meanwhile, Master Penny-Pincher, fearing Ivan had stolen something precious when he left the house, had followed him. Now coming closer, he sees him feasting and wonders where on earth he found a roast chicken and a bottle of wine. But when he sees him counting the gold, unable to contain himself any longer, he cries out in astonishment.

Glancing up, Ivan sees him hiding in the thicket. "Hm!" he says to himself. "Well, let's see if the violin can really do what the old man promised." So he begins to play at a furious pace, and poor Penny-Pincher cannot help dancing. As he is surrounded by thistles and thorns, his whole body is soon scratched and bleeding. "Stop, Ivan!" he shouts. "Please, stop playing! I don't want to dance anymore!" But Ivan fiddles away, at an ever more frenzied pace....

Ah? Maya has already drifted off. Look at her lying there, little black wisps of hair sticking up from her head like a dark crown.... She's fast asleep.

ROBERT

Bad night tonight. She's left the bathroom door half open and I can see she's not well at all. She gulps down one sleeping-pill, then another. Eyes herself mistrustfully in the mirror. Slowly raises both hands and presses them to either side of her head, flattening her hair which is beginning to turn grey. My beloved, my beautiful, aging Lara.

Seeing my reflection in the mirror, she glowers at me and whirls around.

"If Maya is to go to Berlin twice a month," she says, "you're going have to increase our alimony. Plane tickets are expensive."

I'm floored. Why is she talking to me like this? Money has never been an issue between us. Of course I'll manage, I'll find what's needed, that goes without saying — why is she suddenly acting as if we were an ordinary divorced couple, full of mutual suspicion and resentment...?

"Yes, of course, my love," I tell her, looking for some spot on her body that my hand might be able to caress. But she's uncaressable tonight, bristling with invisible quills. "No problem."

"That's your favourite sentence, isn't it, Robert? No problem, no problem — all you have to do is repeat it often enough, then in the end you die and then there *really* is no problem...."

"What on earth is the matter, Lara?"

"Nothing. Do you hear me? *Nothing*... is... the matter!"

"You've been sleeping badly again, your mother tells me."

"I hate it when people discuss me behind my back."

"Lara, please. It's only because we care for you. I *personally* care for you very, very much. If only there were some way I could prove it to you..." and I hold my arms out to her, knowing in advance that the answer will be no.

"No, I don't feel like it. You're right, it's not a good night."

"Have you still got all the prescriptions you need?"

"Yes, Robert. Thank you."

"Well... good night, then."

"Good night, dear."

She kisses me as if I were her brother, then enters her bedroom and shuts the door.

Later, from the room next door where I'm trying to console myself with a detective novel, I hear her moving about, sighing, getting out of bed, going to the bathroom, opening and closing the medicine cabinet.... She's so desperately anxious to sleep.... Is it possible that after all these years, she still goes back to the white room in her dreams? She poured her heart out to me once — I don't remember if it was before or after our divorce. "That's where I knew true happiness," she said, "because I felt needed for the first time in my life. *Someone needed me* — me, and no one else. Life was asking something of me — and for once, there was no doubt in my mind that I could furnish it. It wasn't like the rest... the piano... my mother... even you, Robert.... I didn't sit there worrying whether I'd be good enough — *I was everything I had to be.*"

I've never forgotten those words. They sent shivers running up and down my spine.

The dark house, in the dark garden, the rain still sliding gently down the leaves and branches, rose petals, blades of grass, and seeping into the soil.... Four individuals, four worlds, four flames of consciousness locked away in four different rooms, four lamps blinking on and off in the dark on the house's dark façade, seen by no one.

Maya: sound asleep. Myself: getting lost in the convoluted reasonings of a detective in Manhattan. Lara: tossing and turning in bed.... What about Sofia? What might she be up to, in her room on the top floor?

SOFIA

Thank You, dear Lord. Thank You for helping Maya play well at her audition. I knew You'd answer that prayer for me. I'm truly delighted. Thank You for this scrumptious chocolate bar, too. Forgive me if I don't get up afterwards, to brush my teeth a second time. I just love nibbling a bit of chocolate before I go to sleep, but I haven't the strength to get out of bed again. You understand, don't You? At this stage, it's not my teeth that are going to kill me.

One more thing — if You can, try and make it so that nothing bad happens to Larissa. If You can, eh? I mean, I know You don't get anything for nothing.

Anyway, it was a lovely day. Again, thank You so much. Good night.

LARA

Live, my little one! Breathe, I beseech you! Not only have your eyes begun to focus, but now your tiny hand closes around my finger and squeezes it! — I've never felt anything so exquisite in my life — and before long your lips will be squeezing my nipple, too, won't they, darling? And we'll be able to go home! You'll see.... As soon we get home, I'll introduce you to the pianos. Each has its own temperament, its special qualities and faults: there's Sofia's old Steinway upright on the second floor — we'll move it into your room as soon as you turn three — and in the living room, side by side, two baby grands, a Yamaha and a marvellous Pleyel —

that's the one I love and hate the most. Standing in the kitchen, if you glance over at the Pleyel with its lid propped open, you'd think it was a huge black leaf — or a black petal — or the flounce of a flamenco dancer's black skirt. There's something so... intimidating about that piano's rigid grace, its motionless insolence! One night I dreamed that I opened the Pleyel and my mother was curled up inside it, all shrunken and desiccated, with her eyes shut. It was clear that she was dead, and that the piano was her coffin — but at the same time, I could distinctly hear her voice haranguing me — "I told you music was a matter of life and death," she said — "and you didn't want to believe me. Well, as you make your bed, so you will lie in it! Too bad for you, you'll never be among the chosen few, and you have only yourself to blame."

But *you*, Maya... *never* will you feel guilty when you sit down at a piano keyboard. Your agile little fingers will be filled with joy as they go tearing across the keys at lightning speed! Yes, that's right — squeeze my thumb! Squeeze it hard!

She's doing well, isn't she, Doctor Fabien? She looks good, don't you think? She's making progress.... She'll pull through for sure now, won't she? Do they really need to keep giving her all those shots? I'm so impatient to be nursing her... do you think I'll have to wait much longer? Can't you even give me some idea of when I might be able to take her home? I do everything I'm told, everything I can — I encourage her, I talk to her, I wear a mask so as not to infect her with my germs, my problems, my neuroses.... I swear to you, doctor, I've never even kissed my own daughter!

Er... speaking of germs... would you believe I saw a *butterfly* — *yes, right here*, in the middle of intensive care? I did, I'm sure of it... there was a little white butterfly flitting around the room.... No, no, you're right, of course it's impossible, the room's hermetically sealed and there's no way for insects to get in, I must have imagined it.... Forgive me, Doctor Fabien... I'm so very tired, you understand.... So tired and feverish....

Uncle Lucien is proud as a peacock — a little Romanic church just commissioned three stained-glass windows from him. He starts out with ordinary pencil drawings, and then does a scale model, which he paints in water colours. The dragonfly spends hours hovering around him in his workshop — she's mesmerized by his drawings.

"That guy, there — why's he all doubled over like that?"

"Oh, that's Saint Seraphin. A big, strong, strapping lad — when he was young. He lived out in the middle of the forest and spent all day felling trees and chopping them up into logs. He only slept two hours a night, kneeling on a stone. And in summertime, he made a point of working out in marshlands — so that the mosquitoes would bite him."

"Isn't that called maso-something?"

Lucien laughs. "Nowadays we'd probably call it that, but Seraphin simply wanted to imitate the suffering of Jesus Christ. One day, a band of thieves came into the forest to rob him. And since Seraphin's imitation of Christ included non-resistance to evil, he handed the thieves his only possession — namely, his felling axe."

"Oh, that's great! So they whammed him over the head with it?"

"Exactly. They beat him to a pulp and left him for dead, but he eventually came to and dragged himself back to the monastery.... But for the rest of his life he remained a cripple and walked about hunched over a stick."

"And what about this little baby? Is it baby Jesus? Why's he turning his head away from the Virgin's breast? Doesn't he like her milk?"

"No, no, that's not Jesus, that's Saint Angel. His mother's really old, you see? She was a converted Jew — they say she was so old she could have been his great-grandmother!"

"Oh! So is that why he's turning his head away — because she's so old and ugly?"

"Maya! You should show more respect for your elders.... No. It's because Saint Angel started practising mortification almost as soon as he was born. He did voluntary penance by refusing his mother's breast once a week, every Friday."

"You're making it up... that can't be true!"

"Who knows?... And besides, isn't our capacity for make-believe the pride of our species?"

I'd never dare to contradict Uncle Lucien — he's too well educated and much too kind — but I disagree. I mean, butterflies are good at make-believe, too.... What are homochromia and dissuasive livery, if not artistic lies? Like the *Caligo prometheus*, who proclaims to his enemies, "I'm the head of an owl, I'm gonna eat you!" Or the *Samia cynthia*, which looks like a dreadful dragon! Pride of our species, my eye."

"And what about this one? She's horrible!"

"Ah yes, that's Saint Germaine Cousin, a little shepherdess who lived in the south of France. She was so ugly and deformed that her father and stepmother treated her like a dog, forcing her to sleep out in the stable and feeding her nothing but dry bread. Her job was to tend her father's sheep — but every day she'd go off to mass for two hours and ask God to look after the herd while she was away. And she never lost a single head of sheep!"

"I never dreamed there were so many saints!" says the dragonfly. "The only ones I knew about were the four evangelists and... Saint Joan of Arc!"

"No, there are hundreds of them," says Lucien. "Some famous and some obscure. I love painting the lives of little saints that no one's ever heard of."

At this, the grasshopper leaps to her feet:

"Now I'm gonna tell *you* a story!"

She darts into the next room, sits down at the piano... and a few seconds later, the music starts tickling our eardrums. Never heard anything like it. It's a sort of... presence that enters the room:

there it is, and there's nothing you can do about it.... It's like my silkworms when they start regurgitating their spittle, they rear up on their hind ends and wave their heads around in a figure 8, just the way Lucien is making figure 8's with his badger-hair brush right now, trying to harmonize the light and dark zones — he picks up a thick brush and adds a light coat of grisaille, then uses a thin brush for the faces, then he goes back to the badger-hair brush — in this phase his movements have to be swift and sure, you'd almost think his hands were doing the work by themselves, commanded from afar — not by his brain but by some distant, unfathomable force, just like the worms when they spin those strong threads of the finest silk without even knowing it, and like these notes of music that come dropping out of the sky from another world, so incredibly sure of themselves and of what they've got to say....

All right already, I don't have all day. Gotta go check out my worms and give 'em their chow, gluttonous monsters that they are.

LUCIEN

Annette would have been thrilled to hear her piano played that way. No, I can't say she *is* thrilled — can't give myself the pleasure of imagining her up there watching everything I do and say. Only true believers are lucky enough to live with the dead. We unfortunate modern enlightened lay professors have to make do with our memories.

Amazing child. Hard to believe she's made of flesh and blood. And yet, she's so alive!

If she *could* see me now, Annette wouldn't believe her eyes.... Here I am, surrounded by children, with a thousand jagged bits of coloured glass spread out around me, a mosaic of myriad shapes and stories that coalesce and then dissolve.... A multicoloured journey through the lives of the saints.... Why the Christian saints? she'd ask me, if she were here, but she is not she is not she is not. It's a matter of convenience, I'd tell her. In the world we live in, stained glass is used in churches. And in the country we live in, churches are Christian. So if I want to be able to share your light with other people — but I'm not talking to Annette, I'm just talking to myself — I have no choice but to embrace the local mythology. It's not that hard, really.... Very often, the saints were ordinary men and women of the kind that you admired.

Maya has stopped playing. I can't hear her at all anymore — she must have gone out to join Benjamin in the back yard.

"Anybody home?"

It's her mother... Lara. A fine-looking woman — in her prime, as they say — yet there's something broken about her. She's got these huge, starving, tortured eyes. I'll be friendly, no more. Not the least desire to begin again, try to understand a whole new person. It gets so complicated at our age — we're weighed down by our all accumulated baggage of divorces and deaths, unfulfilled dreams.... The only tales I want to hear from now on are simple ones, as pure and brilliant as my colours. The tales of saints and children. Tales that inspire hope.

"I've brought over a plum pie... well, half a plum pie! I baked it last night, and I thought maybe... for the children's snack...."

"Please sit down," I tell her.

"And some roses from my garden — they were about to burst, scattering their petals all over the lawn!"

"How kind. Yes, they are in full bloom, aren't they?" I will *not* get up to fetch a vase, I despise cut flowers — let her do as she likes with them. But she's welcome to stay and watch me work, yes yes, of course. Why not.

She takes a seat and observes me in silence.

A dangerous thing, silence, between a lonely man and a lonely woman.

"Maya's out back with Benjamin," I tell her. "I think they're measuring silkworms. Did you know their bodies grow a thousand-fold in less than a month? When the eggs are first laid, they're all but invisible; you can stack them in a cigar box by the tens of thousands. But once they start chewing on their mulberry leaves, you can practically watch them grow. A few weeks later, each worm is as big as your thumb — it's really rather staggering. People say kids grow fast, but they're nothing compared to silkworms...."

Good, very good, I'm at all not nervous, glad to say, she's not perturbing me. I go on talking to her calmly, all the while cutting out my bits of glass using the corresponding templates — the three windows require five hundred different pieces so I mustn't get mixed up at this stage. "Your little Maya's a miracle," I tell her. "But you already know that, of course. My wife and I didn't want to have kids — we preferred to go on being kids ourselves, which is to say egotistic and hedonistic. We travelled all over the world together.... But it must be quite something to live with a little magician like Maya.... Did you teach her the piano yourself?"

"I want to kiss you," says Lara. And glancing up, I see she's that sort of person — a person who has nothing to lose, and who doesn't give a damn about appearances, gossip and the rest. Not my type; not my type at all. Annette and I were staunch believers in marriage and monogamy — we took pleasure in conforming to the rites prescribed by our society, since they seemed as good as any others and we knew that humans needed structure of some sort. Still, having no wish to offend this lovely woman, I rise politely and take her in my arms.

The first time, a woman in my arms, since.

Strange. She's the one who kisses me — passionately, I think they used to say — and all it feels is strange. I press her to me, briefly, to let her know I'm about to move away. Then I take a step back and caress her cheek with my finger.

Her eyes are burning far too brightly. How shall I tell her I'm not up to falling in love? I don't mind being polite, but... all I want now is to live the way the saints used to live... in peace... untormented by desire or anxiety. With Annette....

"Forgive me," she says, smiling and lowering her gaze. "You looked so very handsome, sitting there.... I hope you don't mind, I couldn't resist.... It was strange, as if a sort of warmth were emanating from you.... Mmmm, thank you. You're very kind.... Well, I'm off!"

She seems to have gotten the message, as her cheeks pinken prettily and her eyes stop aiming their infinite need at me.... She goes out to the back porch.

"Maya! Don't be too late getting home, dear. You've still got your practising to do...."

Skipping down the back steps, she waves at me and vanishes through the hole in the fence.

BENJAMIN

Squatting down, knees next to ears, the grasshopper pays close attention to my death-dealing operations. She keeps her eyes open and her mouth shut. Most girls are just the opposite, they keep their eyes shut and their mouths open — "Yeeeccchh!" they say, for instance. "That's disgusting!" "That's mean!" and so forth. But Maya's different. Perfectly calm and concentrated. She wants to *understand* the dying; she wants to *see* it. I commit my murders with great gentleness and dexterity because I don't want to damage the specimens. Proud to show her today's trophies: five Provence lemons, two *Parnassius Apollos*, a superb oleander sphinx, even a skeleton sphinx. She's impressed by the delicate movements of my hands as I smother them with the ether.

"Can you *see* it when they die?" she asks. Good question. At first, of course, they're merely knocked out — a bit like human beings under general anæsthesia. Then they kick the bucket, but it's impossible to tell the exact moment at which their souls take off for butterfly heaven....

"What kind of a brain have they got?" Tell the truth, I haven't the slightest idea. She asks pretty smart questions for her age, and especially for her sex.

It blew her away when I told her that silk was made of slobber. "All those beautiful women covered in slobber! That's fabulous!" And she went into gales of laughter — but it was a nice, *real* sort of laughter — not like when the girls at school go into their pseudo-hysterical giggling fits. She found it genuinely funny — and after a while, so did I — that the world's most elegant ladies go prancing around in gobs of slobber secreted by a bunch of ugly worms... As a matter of fact, when you think about it, it's hilarious!

SOFIA

Why can't Larissa leave her daughter alone? Dianescu will soon be taking her in hand — so why can't Maya spend the summer playing as she chooses? Chopin's *Ballade N° 2* is turning into a real battlefield. Listening to them quarrel over it, I can feel my blood pressure shooting up and my heart thumping out the tempo in my head. Calm down, now. Careful, good Lord, I told You I wasn't ready yet. Here... let's heat up a bit of red wine and crush some garlic into it.... *Ahh!* At last I can put up my feet! Blow on the steaming glass.... ouch, it's scalding! One sip at a time, ear to the door....

"But what's Chopin trying to *say* in this passage?" Larissa is asking. "What do you think he wanted to *express?* Don't forget that when you play, you're conveying something, you're sharing it with other people! That's what dynamics are about, and *rubati*, and the rest.... Look, here it says *crescendo*, and here, *diminuendo*; here, you're supposed to slow down a bit before picking up again *a tempo*... You've got to ask yourself what effect he was trying to achieve..."

And she plays the passage in question. Expressively, impeccably, no one can argue with that. But the little one sticks to her guns.

"That's not the way I *hear* it," she says.

"But you're not taking your audience into account! What will *they* be feeling as they listen to you? Music is a sort of... present you can give them."

"I don't know," says Maya. "But to me it sounds better like this!"

And she plays the same passage — flatly, soberly, allowing the notes alone to say what they've got to say, without being coerced by the suffering soul, swept along by torrents of tears, underscored by the pedal. And there's no room for doubt — Maya's rendition is better. Maybe even better than Chopin's, who knows? It is implacable.

Ah, I can feel the garlic wine starting to take effect. This thing is good! The tension may have risen another notch in the next room, but it's finally gone down a bit in my arteries.

LARA

You're so tiny, I'm so tiny, little angel, and the piano is my house, you see — it's a big black castle, and everything's pitch dark inside, just like in your stomach, in my stomach, but it's so *hard*, so *huge*, listen — the hammers come banging down, the noise is deafening — it makes my eardrums thrum and my entire body vibrate, *boom-boom, boom-boom* — yes, it's the beating of my own heart — don't be afraid, Larissa, Maya, don't be afraid, the hammers rise up above me like hideous prehistoric birds, they've been lying in wait for me, getting ready to swoop down, I go running madly along the strings, they hum with electricity, transmitting their vibrations to me — and there are deep chasms between the strings, yawning abysses, but I simply must avoid the hammers — I trip, I'm going to fall, I grab the strings and hang on for dear life, I can't breathe — hang on, my little one, I beseech you, *hang on, breathe!*

SOFIA

Maya goes on playing her implacable *Ballade*, and suddenly Lara can't take it anymore. She rushes into the kitchen to get away from her daughter, not suspecting she's about to run bang up against her mother — oh, poor dear. Well, there's no help for it.

Crossing over to the sink, she turns on the faucet and gulps down a tall glass of water to regain her composure. I pretend not to have noticed what's going on, engrossed as I am in my garlic wine — but the chromatic cascades of the *Ballade N° 2* continue pouring into the kitchen from the living room. Larissa stares at herself in the little mirror above the sink. What does she see?

"Has your blood pressure gone up again?" she asks suddenly, turning to face me. "Are you sure you don't want me to call a doctor?"

"My dear girl," I reply (but she knows my answer off by heart; indeed she's only asked the question to give herself time to recover from the turmoil Maya's playing has plunged her into), "I'll die when the good Lord decides my time has come, and there isn't a doctor in the world who can change that by a minute."

She isn't listening. She sits down across from me at the kitchen table, lights up one of my smooth mellow Balkan Sobranie cigarettes and holds out the elegant flat box to me. For a while, the two of us smoke together in silence.

The *Ballade N° 2* comes to an end. The front door bangs open, then shut. Maya's gone. Off to the neighbours' again.

Silence.

So I decide to take the bull by the horns. I've always believed in frankness.

"My dear Dochenka...."

"What?"

"You're not going to be jealous of your own daughter, are you?"

Larissa goes on smoking in silence. Staring at the table.

And then at last, not looking up, she says in a calm, cold voice, "I will never be jealous of my daughter."

LUCIEN

Saint Martinien had more willpower than I do. He managed to resist temptation every time, the lucky bastard. The world's most beautiful women threw themselves at his feet and begged him to marry them, but God invariably leaped in to save him, just in the nick of time — following which, to sanctify himself, Martinien would sail out to sea and spend years standing alone on a rock amidst the raging main. Where's my rock, Annette? I was sure that the idea of *you* would serve me as a rock for the rest of my days, but.... Oh, I know, you don't hold it against me. I can't even manage to feel guilty. All I feel is weak. Yes. I give in.

Lara has come over every afternoon for the past two weeks. She walks into my studio, watches me work and listens to my crazy saint stories, scarcely opening her mouth, no longer even pretending to be the nice, normal neighbour-lady — no, she just comes over, with her beautiful eyes so full of emptiness, and after a while she moves closer and sinks to the floor at my feet, pressing her body against my legs like a cat; if she were sixteen, this behaviour might seem sweet or charming but at the age of forty-five it means something very different... So, well, I bend down and pet her like a cat, stroking her hair — and then, having ascertained that Benjamin and Maya are indeed out of doors, at the far end of the garden, either dissecting beetles or pushing one another on the swing, I take her to my bed. A bit of tenderness doesn't cost me anything, and she seems to need it so badly. The whole thing is very gentle.

Sometimes she weeps. And afterwards, I cuddle her in my arms as if she were a little girl.

We ask no questions. We confide nothing to each other about our respective marriages. What we are having together is neither a fling nor an affair. Not a part of our life histories. It's beyond the pale, somehow. A strange sensuality, permeated with sadness. I'd prefer... oh, it doesn't really matter. It isn't going to last. A month from now, when September rolls around, everything will sort itself out — Benjamin will go home, Maya will return to school, Lara to the Conservatory, and I'll be left alone at last with my saints and my memories... as I believe I wish to be.

LARA

One monitor follows your heartbeat, another records the rhythm of your breathing, a third keeps track of your temperature, and yet another measures the gas content in your blood. The monitors beat time and we dance with them — it's a waltz, my little Maya! — *one* two three, *one* two three...

But the day will come.

The day will come when, in the middle of rehearsal with the ensemble, my mind will go blank.

Drowning in the whiteness of dawn — everything is white in here — the walls, the ceilings, the clothing, the sheets.... How can I...? What...? Where am I? Which bar were we at, what key were we in, what tempo...? Lost, lost. My fingers on the keyboard.... What am I doing? *What is music? What is music?*

Where were we? Let's take it from 124, for Lara, please. Please, everybody, for Lara please everybody....

I detach my hands from the keyboard and stare at them, engulfed by an absolute, icy blank — *what are* these *for?* My hands are unrecognizable, I have no idea what function they're supposed to fulfill. Oh, it only lasts a few seconds, the other musicians are scarcely aware of it, they get a bit impatient, that's all, they repeat, "Is it okay? Are you with us? Can we take it from 124?"

I have to make an enormous effort to wrench myself back to the page of notes, shake myself out of it, recall the purpose of our meeting.... *Is this music? Are you quite sure?*

ALEXIS

Came for my August lesson with Madame Mestral. At age twenty-four I must be, if not her oldest pupil, at least the one she's been teaching the longest. I have my own pupils now at the Conservatory; maybe even give more concerts than she does — but I still learn a lot from our monthly sessions.

Not today, though. For the very first time, I feel Madame Mestral isn't listening. She's somewhere else. I've launched into a Lisztian delirium, playing like a madman, entirely by heart — and she just sits there, absently, staring out the window. It's insulting.

When the piece comes to an end, she's quite embarrassed. She's got no idea what to say. Suggests I rework this phrasing, that arpeggio. Tries to show me how... and breaks off almost immediately, rubbing her wrists and fingers, complaining of rheumatismal aches and pains... whereas she's far from old.... Her mother, on the other hand, is getting frankly decrepit. She wanders around the house in her slippers, chignon awry, strands of straggly hair floating behind her — I can sense her behind every door, listening in, spying on her daughter and granddaughter.... Yes, the waif with the big dark eyes... the one who was born that memorable afternoon.... What a fool I made of myself that day! I didn't know about the different stages of a delivery. I actually thought Madame Mestral had peed her pants!

This house is beginning to give me the creeps. Maybe I should stop coming for a while. Try to muddle through Liszt on my own.

MAYA

"Mama! Mamochka! Is it all right if Benjamin and Lucien come over for dinner tomorrow night? Wouldn't that be great? Okay? I'm gonna invite them, okay?"

SOFIA

Ah! Always did love a big dinner table.

Ah! Always did love setting the heavy, cast-iron saucepan on the table, removing the lid and hearing the cries of admiration when people see my chicken-and-onion stew and catch a whiff of its aroma. Ages since we've had guests for dinner. This might be the first time since Robert left.

Ah! Always did love the sound of cutlery chinking on plates, mixed up with the sound of voices, the interweaving of different voice colours, men women and children like threads in a tapestry... Reminds me of those Sunday luncheons in Moscow long ago — except the food's better in France, of course. I pour out the wine... and the white-haired man, raising his glass, proposes a toast to Cecilia, the patron saint of musicians.

"They say that she was put to death three days after her wedding for having taken a vow of chastity, and that in that short space of time she'd managed to convert not only her husband and brother-in-law, but even her executioners — and four hundred pagans beside. It's rather baffling. I mean, if everyone had converted, then why did they kill her?"

Maya chatters ceaselessly, brimming over with joy, her eyes burning, sparkling — you'd think it was their electricity that was making her hair stand on end.... The nephew's shy and awkward like all boys his age — he blushes whenever an adult so much looks at him.... Larissa's being charming, or doing her best to be charming, drinking and talking a bit too much.... And the painter neighbour's very amiable, he seems relaxed with her, almost overly nice to me — maybe there's something between the two of them? They avoid meeting each other's eyes, and their voices drop a notch when they speak to each other — oh, good Lord, that would be lovely! Yes, do make them fall in love if You can — it would do Larissa a world of good. But not *too* much in love, if possible — not one of those wild hurricane passions that lay waste to everything in their path. No... a fancy, let's say. Some kisses, caresses, tender looks, that sort of thing. It would be so nice if Lara could have that one more time, before leaving her youth behind her once and for all.

We talk politics. Mister Painter questions me about the Soviet Union. The disproportionate excellence of its musicians. The ransacked churches, the icons that vanished into thin air.... "Didn't anyone think to do what we did here in France — stash the sacred objects somewhere while awaiting better times? During the German occupation, the stained glass was taken out of all the cathedral windows — in Chartres, Bourges, the Sainte-Chapelle — and carefully stored in cellars until the end of the war."

"You must be joking!" I tell him. "The Bolsheviks weren't a foreign army invading us, they were our own children. Hordes of young hooligans in every village! Barging into churches, smashing, trampling, demolishing whatever they could lay their hands on.... And then they stood there and sneered at thé poor peasants's lamentations.... My mother told me. So, you see, we had to learn to turn inwards, and put our faith in invisible things. Words — poems learned by heart, silent prayers. Music. Mathematics. Chess. These were the secret gods of the communist years."

Does me good, to talk.

After dessert, while I'm making the coffee, the white-haired man turns to Maya and says, "Why don't you play something for us on a real piano? You do wonders with our tinny old thing over there, but I'd love to hear the Pleyel close up...."

Maya's delighted. "Sure," she says, "but Mama's got to play, too! Okay, Mamochka? Let's do Schubert's *Fantasia*, okay? Please say yes!"

"Oh," murmurs Lara in a sepulchral tone of voice, lowering her eyes and staring at her hands. "I'm afraid I've had too much to drink, I can't...."

"Sure you can! You can play the *Secondo* if you want, it's easy! Come on, let's show 'em!"

Our two guests exchange glances. They sense that something's wrong. They realize the stakes are higher than....

"Don't make your mother play if she doesn't feel like it," says the painter neighbour. "*You* play something."

"Oh," says Lara, trying to shake out of it. "If it's just the *Secondo* I should be able to handle it...."

No, Dochenka. Don't do it. Leave well enough alone. Let the evening draw to a nice, congenial close. Don't force yourself to confront your demons. Don't do it. There's no point....

But she does it. Walks over to the piano with a heavy step, as if it were a scaffold. I know what my daughter's thinking. *The problem*, she's thinking, *is that the music moves forward, whereas I don't want to move forward. I play it but I refuse to go along with it — I want to hold it back, keep it for myself, press it to my body, squeeze it into a hard ball and stop up my throat with it.*

Now they're seated next to each other, side by side on the bench of the wonderful Pleyel. You've got to be on good terms to play this *Fantasia* — it's an intimate experience. The *Primo*'s left hand is constantly twining between the fingers of the *Secondo*'s right, and the other way around....

Starting off alone, Larissa sets the tempo for the first *Allegro*.... Ah, good, that's fine, I heave a sigh of relief and sit back to listen. The first measures unfold seamlessly, limpidly, with the bass notes as dark and peaceful as a pond in the morning mist, and Maya's melody setting itself off against them, simple and repetitive as birdsong. Then comes the *Largo* with its jagged, ominous chords.... But when that's over, and it's time for the *Allegro vivace*, Maya abandons all restraint. She launches into it at a mad pace — and Lara, realizing it's beyond her powers, begins to stumble after only a few bars.... She hangs in there just the same, doing her best to catch up with her daughter, or at least to seem amused by her defeat.... But all of a sudden she loses it. Her fingers grow entangled, then bog down completely, thumping out several heavy, aberrant chords — then seize up as if in horror, suspended motionless over the keyboard — then flop down into her lap, and stay there.

Maya continues a while by herself, unable to stop, drawn on by the pure pleasure of feeling her fingers caper and cavort upon the keys.... At last she breaks off. Laughing gaily, she throws her arms around her mother's neck and exclaims, "Wow! We sure had fun for a while there, didn't we?!"

And our guests applaud — the clumsy, forced sort of clapping that follows a magnificent failure. Soon they get up to say good-bye.

"Off with you, Maya!" I say. "It's late — have you seen the time? Well past eleven! Go get into your pyjamas, right away! You'll only get a tiny little story out of me tonight."

Snapping out of it at last, Lara rises from the piano bench and begins to clear the table with the movements of a sleepwalker.

MAYA

Well all right, if Babushka's only going to tell me a tiny little story, I'll only play her a tiny little piece — the most microscopic of all Bartòk's *Mikrokosmos* — look, here goes, it starts with next to nothing, you can hardly hear the notes at all, you have to prick up your ears to understand what's going on. It's like a fly, buzzing in annoyance because it just got one of its legs stuck in a spiderweb, and now, darn it, it's getting worse, first one leg stuck then two then three — I'll tell Benjamin about this tomorrow, it'll make him laugh — then the spider comes along — he's this big gangly laid-back Zorro-type, his legs are just about as skinny as his thread — and goes about preparing for the massacre. He wraps up his victim, slowly, lackadaisically, secreting thread as he goes, twisting it round and round the fly like bandages around a mummy.... So, Babushka! How do you like my miniature *danse macabre*? The fly buzzes desperately for help, but then its cries grow fainter and further apart, what we're witnessing is an itty-bitty teeny-weeny torture scene, but still....

What....?

Downstairs... *what?*... Mama's gone back to the Pleyel and thrown herself into Schumann's *Carnival* — flat out — arpeggios scattering all over the place, chords whirling madly — my insects get swept away on her torrents of sound, sucked up in her vortex and drowned....

I can't even hear what I'm playing anymore. So I stop.

"Why's Mamochka doing that?"

LARA

What is music? What is music? What is music? All I know is that *I* am somewhere else, never in the same place it is — my whole life long. I've never known how to make music, all I'm good at is making efforts, years and years of efforts, practising practising practising, writing in the fingering, taking it from the top, trying to get it right, working meticulously and fearfully, striving to "play well," doing my acrobatic best to convey the inner workings of the soul, hearing people say I've got lots of talent — *oh, disparaging phrase!* — and feeling at every instant, behind that talent, raw naked fear.... Whereas it's supposed to be about joy!

My prey. My prayer. Forever beyond my reach.

I'm running across the ice field, I keep tripping and falling in the snow, it's freezing cold out, Maya, murderously cold, and we can't maintain our body temperatures, you'll have to stay in the incubator for the time being, I'll die before I'm allowed to catch up with music.... The piano's so far away... can you see it there in the distance? The beautiful black Pleyel is a mere speck on the horizon, and to reach it I have to cover this vast, open expanse of whiteness.... Then, very gradually, the music arrives and invades everything — sky, ice field, universe — it's deafening, overwhelming, celebrating glorious reconciliations, harvest feasts, the extravagant banquets of the gods — but I'm still down here flailing through the snow, I'll never manage to catch up with it....

You'll find it, though, Maya, without even having to look for it. You'll play as if you had neither hands nor piano — as if, reaching out, you touched not the keyboard but *music itself*! As if you were dancing on the tightrope of heaven! Yes, my love — because — you'll never come completely down to earth. You'll always stay in touch with the limbo you lived in during your first months. You'll take the vibrations of the cold machines and turn them into Bach fugues; ecstasy will be the air you breathe.

Looking at you, listening to you, it's clear that you're not one of us. You're not weighed down with human earth and clay. No. You're not playing for our sake. You're playing for the sake of music.

SOFIA

Listen, God. You really shouldn't let things degenerate like this. I've got no idea what You might be cooking up for us, but I have to say it doesn't smell too good. And I won't be around forever to smooth things over.

Ah. So tired. Dead tired. I can feel the accumulated burden of the years in every particle of my flesh.... This earthly frame has grown inordinately heavy — pretty soon I won't be able to lug it around anymore.... No wonder we dream of leaving it behind and recovering the weightlessness of angels. *What is music?* Who said that? *Music is like the word farewell on the lips of an old man.* Can't remember. So many quotations cluttering up my memory now.... Pigsty memory, garbage-dump memory....

All I ask is that You leave Maya's talent alone. Okay? You've given her such a perfect gift, don't let it be harmed by vicissitudes, the gnawing rats of reality, please. I know You can be a quite a prankster when You set your mind to it. I still haven't forgotten Olga, Seriojka's accompanist, who received the whole weight of a grand piano on her left hand. A piano she was helping to move, because at the time there wasn't supposed to be any difference between artists and musclemen. Amputation of the index and middle fingers. I'll never forget the day she came out of hospital and greeted me wordlessly by holding up her mutilated hand.... Oh yes, I know! These trials You send us always are meant to teach us something — patience, transcendent faith, so on and so forth.... Well, God, if You ask me, I think I've been extremely patient and reasonable all these years; I've spent my whole life wishing and praying for just this sort of miracle — Maya's talent — and now that it's finally happened, I suggest You just avert Your gaze and go busy Yourself with something else for a few decades. All right?

ROBERT

Never called me in the middle of the night before. The telephone ripped my dream apart — like a siren, like the signal of every emergency in the world, fires, assassinations, riots, German bombing raids, nuclear catastrophe — I wonder what this corresponds to in the brain, which part of the cortex is stimulated by that strident throbbing to inform us that *something's wrong....*

Somewhere in the world, something is wrong.

Nathalie was very annoyed. "This time your ex has gone too far. Has she no respect for our privacy? Has she forgotten that the judge pronounced your divorce *eight years ago?* Why does she always turn to *you* for help? Why can't she call an ambulance, or a girlfriend, or a crisis support service? Why does it have to be *you?* And at one in the morning this time! Where does she get off? *Don't go,* Robert, I'm warning you. If you go, you'll be sorry..."

I come anyway, of course, leaping into my Alfa and gulping down thirty-five miles of black highway in half an hour. I haven't got any choice. Lara's an absolute in my life, that's the way it is. I can't explain it, and I can't justify it.

The siren was telling the truth. Something's wrong indeed. I find Lara curled up in her nightgown in an armchair, chain-smoking. She's got her legs crossed — no, knotted; there's a knot in her throat, too, and the incoherency of what she says dismays me.

LARA

Oh, to sleep! To hold you again, Maya, my tiny baby! I've always hated mornings, the return of daylight. Schumann understood that much, Robert, oh, dear Robert, whose *Songs of Dawn* were songs of madness written in the asylum. Every day, every day, the moment of waking an unspeakable disappointment. Having to abandon sleep — with its wealth of colors, dimensions, significations — for the poor pallor of reality, where we have no choice but to put one foot stupidly in front of the other.... Every morning, the Fall. Banished from Eden; condemned to drag our weight, our nakedness and pain throughout the day. *Where* to take refuge? *Why* wake up? What right have they to force me...? I've always sympathized with roosters, who scream bloody murder at the first glimmer of dawn. I, too, feel like screaming when I realize the sun's about to rise. It's outrageous, being brought back to the here and now. I so long to be back *then*, in the whiteness of the walls and sheets, the translucency of skin, the warmth of my gaze on the tiny infant I'm pressing to my chest, rocking with and talking to — the child who needs me. Only sleep can take me back to her. And sleep eludes me.

I can't stand hearing her anymore! Five, six, seven hours a day, music flows from her fingers — a limpid, luminous waterfall of notes, indefinitely renewed.... Oh God, where did all this clear running water come from — all these clear running notes? Will they never cease? If I promise her ten thousand meringues, a ton of chocolates, a vat of lemonade — will she finally stop playing? Or at least break off long enough for me to catch my breath?

Advancing... forever advancing... inexorably.... Her melodic lines don't sing together; don't reach out to each other; they neither console the heart nor caress the eardrum. Each of them is sovereign and pitiless — insolent in its individual perfection. Her music is suffocating me, it's choking up my soul — it's killing me! Such beauty! Sumptuous and simple. Transparent and autonomous. Utterly free. A beauty that knows nothing of who we are, cares nothing for our cramped and crooked destinies. A beauty we'll never be able to really hear or grasp. Because it... passes. Because it *is* the past — a piece of flimsy gossamer lace, spun between us and nothingness. Intolerant, intolerable beauty. The gaping wound... and the soothing balm for the wound. Pure time. Pure mortality. Coming into being, then vanishing without a trace. Like... me. My heart beats out the rhythm; it beats and beats — and what for? So as to stop beating. So that silence can at last return to silence. We're hardly even here. Our days are numbered. Look how fast they tick away! We're dying, all of us! Music helps us forget this fact, and at the same time makes it inescapable.

Oh... the metallic taste of this world. An end-of-the-world sort of taste. Tungsten on the tongue.

ROBERT

"Lara," I say to her. "Lara, my love. My darling."

For hours, I repeat the same words to her over and over again. I stay with her until dawn, holding her hands in mine and stroking her cheek, unwet by any tears. I kiss her lips, her forehead, the nape of her neck; her skin is burning hot.

"Lara, my Lara, don't torment yourself like this. You're exhausted, my love — that's why everything looks so black. You need a change of scene." I know my vocabulary is limited, inadequate; I know it isn't a question of scene. What needs to be changed? Life... the world... I don't know how to put it into words. I don't have the means — I'd have to be a poet, not a biologist.... The intensity of what's going on here is too much for me. But I continue as best I can: "You should get away for a while," I suggest. "Take as long as you need. I could come and stay here, I'd look after Maya, you wouldn't have to worry about a thing."

"No, no," she says. "No. I've got to work it out of myself."

Odd, her saying "of" instead of "by myself." But I don't ask her about it, because all at once she sags against my chest, as if about to faint. Deeply moved, I take her in my arms and carry her over to the bed. It's so easy to help her take off her nightgown, get undressed myself and and to lie down with her — for her, in the bed. There's not the least haste or clumsiness in our movements. As I move onto the body of my wife, I am hard, needed, urgent. She knows how to find me and be there for me, with me, she always has. Moaning, I slowly descend into the wilderness through which she's wandering. "Lara! Lara!" I cry out as our two bodies glide together, mingling their sweat and their chagrin.

Never will I understand human copulation. I find it baffling that such a banal and functional act, theoretically intended for the reproduction of the species, can thus suck up the soul and send it hurtling out of this world...

MAYA

This morning I'm going to give Babushka a real treat. She won't believe her ears — between nine and eleven thirty, Bach's *Sixth Partita* off by heart, the whole thing, note perfect. Babushka is rocking back and forth in her rocking chair. As usual, she pretends not to be paying attention to me — just day-dreaming, you know, like an old lady who's not all there anymore — but I know she's listening with all her might. She doesn't miss a single trill, a single shading of dynamics.

Not bad, eh? What do you think?... I'm hardly using the pedal at all — who needs it? Listen, Babushka! The notes are filing out on stage to dance, just for you!

Ah, you see? Isn't that great? The *Toccata*'s already down pat. I don't even have to think about what I'm doing — I'm like that little butterfly flitting around your head, wonder how it got through the window, did it float into the room on a sunbeam?... Maybe it came in through the back door when Mama went out to tend to her roses.

She'll make us a beautiful bouquet today, you can be sure of that!

Mmm, what a gorgeous day, sunlight pouring in from all directions. I just love summertime — don't you, Babushka? You must be glad to be living in the south of France now, instead of your frozen old Russia! Still, I love listening to your tales of ice and snow. Especially the one about the drunkard, it makes me laugh every time I think of it; when your parents were coming home from a concert one December night, it was past midnight and the temperature was forty below zero, that's unbelievable, *forty below!* Your mama rushed right into the house but all of a sudden your papa saw this drunkard lying sound asleep in the snow at the edge of the road! So he ran over to him and started pulling on his arm. "Come on!" he said. "Wake up, come into the house, you mustn't stay here, you'll freeze to death!" But the guy didn't wake up, he must have been dead drunk because he didn't even budge, maybe he'd already frozen to death, his arm was as stiff as wood but your papa kept pulling at it, harder and harder, shouting, "Wake up!" — and suddenly he pulled so hard that the arm came off in his hands. "*Masha!*" he screamed to your mother, who'd come back out to see what was holding him up. "*MASHA! I'VE KILLED HIM!*"... whereas in fact it was a prosthesis — that's when I learned the word 'prosthesis' — it really *was* a wooden arm. That's so great, I love that story, even if I don't know how it ends because everybody is always laughing so hard they forget to ask what happened next, whether the drunkard finally woke up or what.... Anyway, Bach's music always reminds me of summertime. I've never understood how people could say it was cold, to me a Bach fugue is the warmest thing in the whole world — don't you think so, Babushka? It's like when Mama's lying on the couch reading a book and I come and curl up next to her...

Oh, that butterfly is getting on my nerves! How am I supposed to concentrate if it keeps flitting around my head? I'd give it to Benjamin as a gift but I don't know how to catch it without crushing it. Maybe I should try to shoo it out the window... Babushka?

She never sleeps when I'm playing. She rocks, she smokes, she stares out the window, maybe thinks about the story she's going to tell me at bedtime... but she never sleeps. "Babushka?"

Ah. So it's that. Babushka.... Are you dead, my Babushka?

I come up very close to see. Her head has dropped forward. Yes, that must be it. You're dead. It's all over. The snowy nights of

Moscow are gone forever. I love you, my Babushka. Where was I — in the middle of the *Sarabande?* Listen...

Then Mama comes back from the garden with her arms full of flowers. Poor Mama. She doesn't know it yet, but they're flowers for a funeral.... Suddenly her movements change. She must have seen. She rushes over to the rocking chair to make sure. No pulse, no breath, nothing. Now she's sure.

"Maya!" she says in a low voice. "Maya... your grandmother has just died."

I nod my head, but I want to play the *Partita* off by heart all the way through, the way I promised Babushka I would. I want to keep them together in my heart forever.

"For the love of God, Maya! Have you no respect? *Stop playing the piano!* How *can* you.... I tell you your grandma's dead... and to you it makes *no difference whatsoever?*"

Bursting into tears, she rushes out of the room, and I come after her. I find her slumped at the kitchen table with her head on her arms. The flowers she just picked are scattered all around her.

"Mamochka — forgive me... but to me, that *was* respect..."

LUCIEN

Another smoky funeral service. Remember Benares, Annette? Remember all the chaos and confusion of our day in Benares? Humanity wallowing in all its fleshly extremes at the same time — wading through mud and excrement and ashes, thousands of people squatting at the edge of the Ganges, performing their ablutions or defecating, thousands of others wading in up to their necks in the same sacred water to purify themselves — and on the riverbanks, rows and rows of funeral pyres on which dead bodies were slowly burning — and, a mere few steps away, sprawled amidst the crowd of lepers, beggars, wild-eyed old men and starving children, a woman grunted and wept in the effort to give birth.... The irreality of the scene was heightened by the sharp, stifling, ubiquitous smoke of burning wood and flesh — to say nothing of the tumult of cries, lamentations, chanted prayers — a vision of Hell or simply of this Earth — the basic, unadorned existence of human beings, stripped of the reassuring apparel in which our own culture dresses it....

In the Western world, life's various facets are carefully circumscribed. There's a place for giving birth, another for defecating, another for praying and yet another for dying.... I remember, Annette, trying hard not to notice how effortlessly the undertakers carried your coffin through the church. It weighed almost nothing, most of your flesh having already melted away.... Lara's mother was pretty hefty, though. A formidable little lady. There are not many people here to weep for her today. Robert and Lara — sitting side by side and holding hands like an old couple. Benjamin — squirming with boredom, not even a termite in which to sink his mental teeth. Little Maya — staring straight in front of her with a look of intense concentration on her face, as if she were trying to make out something beyond the heavy smoke of candles and incense, beyond the extravagantly gilded altar. Apart from the immediate family, there's scarcely a handful of friends and acquaintances.... But the choir... I'm sure Sofia would have loved the choir. Gregorian chants. The deep, dark sonorities of those male voices, rising *a cappella* from the netherworld and interweaving in the air, in a tight mesh that will wrap itself around her soul and waft it away to its final destination.

Whatever would we do without these images, Annette? Who cares if we don't believe in life after death? Metaphors help us to get through life *before* death, which is already something!

One by one, we are departing. My mother. My father. One of your brothers, two of my cousins and... how many friends already? Then you. Yes. You too, my love, have departed. And no one cries out in indignation. All of us hold our tongues. That's the most incredible thing of all. Shattered by the pain of their successive losses, old people become more and more silent. They allow the young to go on blathering — just as *they* used to blather, when they were young. Ah, this is not what we'd expected, is it? Naturally, we knew that everyone had to die. But we had no idea how much it would hurt, every time. The shock leaves us breathless. Speechless. Helpless.

When my day comes, I'd like to die like Saint Thecle. She lived all by herself in a cave near Selecia, and was so gifted at healing that sick people flocked to her from far and wide, and the local physicians lost all their clientele. Furious, they came thundering up the mountainside to lay hands upon her — but she ran over to a large rock which promptly split open, then sealed itself shut behind her — end of story; a happy ending.

BENJAMIN

The flea doesn't bother me; she actually listens when I explain things to her. It's fun explaining things to people who really listen — maybe I should think about being a professor of entomology and not just an entomologist.

She's not the least bit squeamish — and not chicken, either. She lets me put earthworms, caterpillars and ants in the palm of her hand. Most girls draw the line at ladybugs. Like my little sister Poupette — she was riding her bike last summer, a butterfly landed on her wrist and she got so hysterical she let go of the handlebars and fell flat on her face. Unfortunately Mom was coming right up behind her and couldn't stop — so Poupette got a big red scrape across her back, all the way from her right hip to her left ear — just because of a harmless little *Boarmia roboraria!*

Anyway, not only does Maya-the-Bee pay attention when I explain things to her, she shows amazement when they're amazing. Like when I told her that grasshoppers have ears on their knees, or that midges crawl under the eyelids of water-buffaloes to drink their tears, or that the light of a firefly will die out if you take it too far from home — she was goggle-eyed. I praised her enthusiasm.

"It's good not to be blasé," I told her. "Do you know what 'blasé' means?"

"No!" she answered.

She's truthful, too... which is even *more* unusual!

"Blasé's when nothing can surprise you."

"Oh, yeah! My grandma had a remedy for that. When she thought people didn't seem surprised enough by what she was telling them, she'd say, 'And what about the white horse in the bathtub? Have you seen *that?*'"

Funny little flea. Today, my precious *Bombyx mori* being fully grown, and having shed their skins four times, I'm going to give her the unique honour and privilege of watching them spin their silk.

"Look.... they're starting to make their cocoons. See that?"

"Wow!"

"Sh-sh-shhh.... Don't disturb them."

"You really think they can hear us?"

"Are you kidding? Of course they can! They're extremely delicate, sensitive little critters. In silkworm-breeding houses, they're treated like real princesses. I read somewhere that they can't stand flies, or dogs, or the smell of garlic...."

"Then we better not take them to our place — my grandma liked garlic so much the kitchen still reeks of it!"

"Look how fast they work," I say. "When they're in good shape, they can cough up a foot of slobber a minute — isn't that incredible?"

"A whole foot?" The mosquito's getting excited.

"Yeah. And by the time they're done, there's more than half a mile of silk thread in every cocoon."

"No — *HALF A MILE!*"

I really like her spontaneity. It isn't fake, either. She's right — when something's incredible, you should say so... But just then, the lady next door sticks her head through the hole in the fence.

"Maya darling.... I'm going to go pick up a loaf of bread, I'll be right back...."

"Could you get us some meringues too? Please, Mama! Please! It's been ages since we had meringues!"

"All right, if they have any. See you later — you should come home pretty soon and set the table."

"Okay, I will. Soon as Benjamin finishes showing me his silk-worms."

I like the way she takes me seriously — makes me feel good.

"And now," I tell her, once her mom has gone, "we've got an important choice to make. It's art or life. You decide. Can't have it both ways."

"What do you mean?"

"Well... if you let the worm become a butterfly, it'll tear its cocoon apart and destroy the silk. If you want to keep the silk, you've got to bump off the worm."

"How do you bump it off?"

"You stifle it with hot air."

"Does it hurt?"

"You mean you don't want to hurt a caterpillar?"

"No, it isn't that. I just want to know what we're doing."

"I don't have the faintest. You can't hear it scream, if that's what you mean. So? What do you prefer?"

"Well, maybe we could kill half of them, and keep the other half to see the butterflies?"

"That's fine with me.... But I can tell you the butterflies are nothing to write home about. I've seen them before — bunch of flitty little white things is all."

"It doesn't matter. They'll remind me of my grandma."

"Okay, if you say so. Personally I don't see the resemblance, but if you say so.... So, ready...? Okay, let's go!"

LARA

So I'll walk out into the street, my angel. That day.

And everything, everything will be so strange. I know it's still the same summer — a summer evening like any other, yes I do know that, my sweet — but somehow it's different. My feet don't quite touch the ground as I walk, and the shapes and outlines of things are far too distinct; when I look up at the trees, I can see each and every leaf sharply delineated against the sky, I'm aware of every breath I take, every one of my footsteps on the sidewalk, I seem to be floating, weightless, and though I've lived in this neighbourhood for twenty years it's dreamlike somehow — as if each house were a poignant memory come back to life — everything's so moving — yes, that's it, I'm *moved*, overcome with nostalgia — as if I didn't really have the right to be here — as if I'd been granted a special favour, the privilege of walking on the earth. The Human Planet. I murmur this under my breath: "This is the Human Planet," I say. Everything seems excessively beautiful and makes me want to weep — the street lamps flickering on in silence, the various sounds of a day drawing to its close, the houses so familiar yet so foreign, almost unreal, the women bustling about in their kitchens, the men washing their cars or having a chat at the back fence.... And then, out of the corner of my eye, what should I see — or think I see — but... the fox! You saw it, too, Maya, I remember, on the day of your audition.... It must be a sign.

I arrive at the bakery, light-headed, light-footed — it's only me, I feel like saying, yes, it's only me, a woman like any other, standing in line, awaiting her turn, the baker-lady smiles at me — ah, so she recognizes me! — but her smile makes me want to weep, as does the sight of the other customers — all these people asking for bread, or rolls, or *baguettes* — such comforting, familiar words for such wonderful, basic, irreplaceable things — the flour baked in the oven to fill our stomachs and bring us happiness — now I'm at the front of the line and I say, "A whole wheat loaf, please," and the baker-lady turns round, takes a loaf from the shelf, wraps it in a piece of white paper and hands it to me without a word — oh, we understand one another, there is no need for words — both of us know that something sacred is taking place here, the bread is warm in the palm of my hand and I say, "I'll take a pound of chocolate meringues as well." The baker-lady's smile broadens, I can even see her teeth. She says, "Feel like spoiling your little one today, eh?" and I'm not sure whether or not it's an accusation, does she really think I'm spoiling you? I lower my gaze to rummage for the coins in my change-purse and suddenly I have the feeling the light has changed, there's an ominous shadow just above my head, making it hard for me to look back up at the baker-lady — but no, nothing has changed, she takes my coins and drops them into the cash register, I hear them chink against the coins that are in there already — and it sounds so beautiful, like a jaunty piece of music — everything's grown beautiful again, so I say, "Thank you, have a nice evening," and I leave the bakery.

At first I head for the house, my darling; truly I do. But when I get to the corner, I see a man sitting on the sidewalk. An unshaven man of uncertain age, dressed in rags and tatters, holding out his hand to me. I stand there hesitating, staring at him. He looks so sad. Is he inviting me to dance with him? No, that isn't it — I remember now, people who sit in the streets are *hungry!* He must be hungry, the poor man. So I give him the bread. I give him the bread, and then I think — but that will never be enough! He'll still be hungry afterwards! So I give him the meringues, too. That way, I tell myself... that way... and then I have no idea which way. I'm lost. I scarcely hear his surprised thanks as I move off.... I turn a corner and start to walk. In any direction. It's dark now, and I go on walking.

Later, feeling weary, I enter a café downtown.

"Bye, Lucien! I'm off!"

"You're going home?"

"Yup!"

"Be sure to stop by tomorrow; I'll be taking my three little saints out of the oven, piecemeal. At the moment, they're getting their bottoms seriously warmed — look, it's seven hundred degrees Celsius in there! That'll give them an idea of what they escaped from!"

"What?"

"No, nothing. So, anyway — see you tomorrow!"

"Right... Bye!"

And I slip through the hole in the fence. Quick quick because I'm late, Mama must be back already, I promised her I'd set the table and then I couldn't tear myself away from the silkworms. Hope she's not angry.

"Mama?"

Hm. That's funny. No answer. What time is it?

Eight-thirty. Hm.

I turn on all the lights and set the table.

I'm hungry. I go get a piece of cheese out of the fridge. Since there's no bread to eat it with, I sit down on the couch and nibble at it like a mouse. One of Papa's little white mice... That was so funny when he said he'd make a cat out of Swiss cheese. The house is quiet.

I go outside. It's really getting dark now. I walk down to the gate and peer out into the street to see if Mama's coming. Nope. She's not.

I drink a little milk. Then I sit down at the piano. Bach's *Chromatic Fantasy in D minor*. The piano feels better. It was getting a bit nervous, there. It's not used to the house being so quiet so early in the evening. The piano and I tell each other stories, the way Babushka and I used to do. I feel all right.

The phone rings. I know it isn't her.

"Hello?"

"Is that Maya Mestral?"

"Yes...."

"Dianescu speaking. I hope you still intend to come for your first lesson in September?"

"Yes of course, sir."

"Well, I'm putting my fall schedule together. I was just calling to discuss the exact date with your mother."

"Ah.... Unfortunately, she had to go out tonight. She told me she'd be home quite late."

"Could you ask her to get in touch with me before the end of the week?"

"Yes, sir.... Before the end of the week, I'll tell her."

"If I happen to be out, she can make arrangements with my secretary. You won't forget, will you?"

I go back and sit down again at the piano, but without playing. I stare at the keyboard. It's really beautiful... all black and white... it looks sort of staid and dignified, like a penguin or a man in a tuxedo. From the outside, you'd never guess at all the secrets it has in it! Hmm....

I go back to the *Fantasy*. The fugue starts out so peacefully, like somebody walking, one step after another, and then the other voices come in one at a time and start dancing, adding on trills and chords, it gets more and more complex, each voice speaks out in turn, trying to make itself heard above the others... oh, it's fantastic....

LARA

I sit down in the café, order a glass of red wine and drink it like a woman in a film — you know, like a woman who's just arrived in a foreign city where she doesn't know a soul. I'm having a good time, Maya! But all of a sudden, a wave of fatigue washes over me and I lurch to my feet.

I must sleep.

I must have a bed, at once.

Coming out into the street, I see a neon sign blinking on and off: "HOTEL," it says. Isn't that incredible? All I have to do is think the word "bed," and a hotel materializes before my very eyes — it's like magic, I tell myself, it's a sign from above, it means I'm really meant to enter this hotel, I haven't got a choice. But at the same time, you see, it makes me nervous. Because in my other existence, I was a professor at the Conservatory, a woman who was known and respected throughout the city — and in this new, film-like existence, here I am walking into a squalid little hotel, maybe even a whorehouse. The man at the desk greets me indifferently, scarcely glancing up from his newspaper. He does not stare at me in bewilderment. He agrees to each of my requests and hands me a key, asking neither for proof of my identity nor for any explanation of my presence here. I wanted a bed, and a bed shall be given me. I'm unspeakably grateful to this man. I want to fall to the ground and cover his feet with kisses, anoint them with tears of gratitude — but he has already stuck his nose back into his newspaper.

So I get into the elevator.

MAYA

Now it's too late. It's nearly midnight — Mama wouldn't call this late, she'd be afraid of waking me. My mother's such a kind person, she's always sensitive to other people's feelings — I love her so much. Oh, I might as well sit next to the phone, just in case. Oh, I might as well pick up the receiver, just in case. I listen with all my might, but all I can hear is the high A of the dial tone. I recognized it right away, at age two, when I picked up a receiver for the first time. Vocal groups use it in practice sessions, if nobody's brought a tuning fork. They pick up the phone — *la-a-a* — and that's it, they can start singing!

You sang to me, didn't you, Mama? In intensive care, you told me, the other "premas" had little stuffed animals with them in the incubator, or one of their mother's scarves, or some other piece of clothing with her smell on it, some parents even put a Bible or a Koran in the incubator with their babies — I wonder how the doctors could have sterilized *that!* But I had your voice. It kept me company from the day I was born. It gave me life and music at the same time — and I can still hear it, right this minute.... *You'll go hide under the piano and it'll be your house, your log cabin — everything around you will vibrate when I play,* boom, *the low notes, the pedal — a storm, a deluge, a hurricane of music, raging through the woods!*

LARA

I don't feel like sleeping anymore. I just want to be here. In the city.

I don't turn on the lights. I stand at the window smoking a cigarette and staring out at the city lights. Street lamps, headlights, blinking neon signs... there's something terrible about it, something so hopeless... as if all these lights were signals, people calling for help in a code I can't understand. Cities never sleep. People wander around in them — restlessly, incessantly — like thoughts in the brain. They skulk this way and that, not even knowing why. I go on smoking.

Then I feel my head spinning. I've had nothing to eat since this morning. I sink onto the bed near the window and stare blankly at the white sheet, livid in the light of the street lamp. Yes, it's the white room again. Everything is white and sterile. I go on smoking, and an ember falls from my cigarette onto the sheet. It makes a little black hole as it goes out — like the bullet hole in the forehead of a man who's just been shot. I take my cigarette and make another hole on purpose, just so the first one won't feel lonely. Then another and another. Lots of little dancing, singing hole notes... but now they're getting out of hand, the notes are falling all over each other, spilling off the staff — out of the bed, the room, off the edge of the Earth! I can hear them... They're all trying to say something but it doesn't make sense at all. Look, look! A, C, F, B-flat... it's abominable! The notes are everywhere, randomly scattered across the cosmos — oh, I never wanted this!

MAYA

Must have fallen asleep... hm! Guess I spent the whole night on the couch. Well, that way I won't waste any time getting all undressed and dressed again — just run a comb through my hair — and it's tomorrow!

Milk... bowl of corn flakes.... Hello, world!

BENJAMIN

"Hi!"

"Hi!"

The kid's over early this morning — looks about as crumpled and rumpled as a larva before nymphosis. She must be impatient to see the little saints coming out of the oven in bits and pieces. Yeah, they're baked to a crisp.... "Only after firing," Uncle Lucien tells her, "does the enamel reveal its color. When you first paint it on, it can be anything from black to blood-red, but if you want it to tell the truth, you have to torture it, bring it to white heat... a bit like the saints themselves, come to think of it!" He's trying to make the dragonfly laugh. She pretends to be listening to everything he says, but I can tell she's not as alert as usual. The way she nods her head is sort of automatic. Then all of a sudden, she gives me a big wink and glances out at the back yard. Okay, meet you there in five minutes. What's up?

"Benjamin," she says in a low voice — but not exaggeratedly low, not like she was making a big thing out of it — "I have a secret."

"Yeah?"

"It's a really important secret. I'm gonna tell you, but you have to swear not to tell anyone else. Do you swear?"

"Uh... sure."

"Say: I swear."

"Uh... I swear."

Taking a deep breath, she stares hard at me for a second, then looks away towards the swing. Finally she whispers, "My mother's gone. I'm alone in the house."

"Oh!" I say. "Where'd she go?"

"I can't tell you that. All I can tell you is that we have to leave her alone. We can't bother her. Do you love me?"

Just like that, out of the blue, *Do you love me?* I feel a weird fluttering in my chest, but I say, "Uh... sure."

"You love me. So is it a deal? You won't tell anyone?"

"Uh... How long do you think she's gonna be gone?"

"Oh, not very long.... It'll be fun — you'll see! It'll be our secret... just like Huck Finn, when he runs away and takes the old slave Jim along with him.... You'll look after me, won't you? You'll take care of me?"

"Uh... sure," I say, feeling like an idiot for answering *Uh... sure* every time she asks me a question.

"Anyway, for now let's just keep on playing, okay? As if nothing had happened."

So we spend the whole morning crawling around the garden looking for beetles, we're having so much fun that when Uncle

Lucien comes out on the back porch it feels like only about fifteen minutes have gone by; we can't believe it's already noon....

"Lunchtime! Wanna stay and have lunch with us, Maya?"

"Yeah, I'd love to! I'll just make sure it's okay with Mama!"

Not even glancing at me to see if I'm impressed by her nerve — I'm impressed, I'm impressed — she dashes home and back in thirty seconds: "Mama says it's okay, I can stay!"

I'm impressed.

LUCIEN

"Go wash up, you grimy little imps! Just look how dirty you are!"

I refrain from telling them the story of Saint Psote, who was always as fresh and clean as a new penny (his physical cleanliness being the reflection of his pristine soul, of course); you could lock him up in a pigsty with muck and dung up to his waist, or plunge him into the cesspool and leave him there for twenty days — he'd emerge smiling and immaculate, smelling of roses. No, I will *not* tell them this story.

"Tomatoes? Some paté? How about some cheese? Another slice of bread?" Little Maya eats ravenously, devouring everything I put on her plate and refilling her mouth before she's chewed what's in it. I've never seen her with such an appetite.

We chit and we chat. We talk about Benjamin's plans for the future. About his high school — he'll be entering tenth grade this fall. About his many siblings. About his father's unemployment benefits. You see, Annette? It's quite possible to go on living, even after the unthinkable has occurred. You just have to stay very close to what's right there in front of you — the children, the chit-chat, the food, the wasps, the way the sun glints off the crystal water pitcher — and give it your approval, second by second. That's what life is all about.

Then the sprite asks me, out of the blue, "Do you believe in God?"

I'm sitting there stirring a lump of sugar in my coffee cup, all nice and cozy with the idea of Annette in my head, and Maya goes and asks me a question like that. Reminds me of her mother, the day she said *I want to kiss you.* The spoon leaps from my hand and clatters to the floor.

"Who, me?" I say, bending to pick it up under the table, grateful for a moment's delay... and for the head-down posture as an excuse for my flaming cheeks.

Benjamin's waiting to see what kind of an answer I'll come up with. He's curious — nervous, too — knows his father and I don't see eye-to-eye on the subject.

"Uh... God? Which god?"

"The good one, of course!" says Maya, laughing. "You know, good God, good Lord — the one my Babushka used to talk to all the time."

"Well, er, I guess so," I say at last. "A good God — sure, why not? I've got no problem with that. I wouldn't put stock in a God who lives way up in the sky, beyond life or after it. But a here-and-now God, sure. I can go along with that. In fact I see him everywhere. In people's eyes, or my stained-glass windows, or a meal shared with friends, or your music.... "God" is when people realize they're alive... and that it's not something they should take for granted — right?"

"But do you pray to him?"

"No, I don't pray. But I have nothing against prayers, as long as they're real ones. Like when people bow their heads at the beginning of a meal to say look, we're all here together, we've got food on the table and we're glad of it. We're grateful for this unique moment.... Yeah, that seems to me a good sort of prayer. My wife was the like that...."

"What?" exclaims Maya in surprise. "You mean you're divorced, too?"

"No, no. I'm a widower. Isn't that an ugly word? I always thought it sounded like some ghastly bird cry — *Wi-do-wer, Wi-do-wer!* My wife was totally hung up on daily life. She could turn a ride on the Paris subway into a grand adventure. She'd close her eyes, listen to the sound of the engine, feel the train start to gather speed, hear its hum rise swiftly into the high notes, and she'd sit there, shaking her head in wonder at this astonishing fact: *We're travelling! Do you realize that?* We're being transported from here to there, from Châtelet to the Hôtel-de-Ville in no time at all! Fast and smooth and streamlined, the train goes whizzing along its gleaming rails without a bump or a jerk — bravely defying, piercing, cleaving the darkness of the reinforced concrete tunnel — yes, here we are, sixty feet below the surface of the earth and yet flooded with light, reading novels, talking with friends or even listening to music! After a while, our miraculous vehicle starts to slow down; its loud hum softens, then lapses into silence. The train has arrived at its destination; it ejects some of its passengers onto the platform, safe and sound, and allows new ones to embark for the next leg of the trip — the next chapter of the story — from the Hôtel-de-Ville to Saint-Paul!

Maya shrieks with laughter — and even Benjamin, who's not the shrieking type, allows a big grin to spread over his face.

"Well, if that's what it means to believe in God," says Maya, "then *I* believe in him, too!"

With that, she leaves the table, skips off into the next room and starts banging away on the piano — a wonderfully rhythmic, dancing piece — some sort of jig, I suppose. Unbelievable.

ALEXIS

What an odd coincidence. Last night I was about to call Madame Mestral to cancel today's lesson, but I didn't have the nerve;

today I get here and the waif tells me her mother is out. Something came up. She told the waif to tell me she was sorry. Promised she'd telephone to set up another date. It isn't fair. I take three different buses, I come all the way across the city, I get here on time, never a minute late — and she can't even bother to be here. Could have picked up her phone, for Chrissake. This is intolerable. No, I've made up my mind — it's time to break it off.

MAYA

Getting dark again — like yesterday, like every day. The earth keeps turning, so night has no choice but to fall, that's just the way it is.

Two days can never be the same. Any more than the fugue can be the same today as it was yesterday. It's a new piece of music every time you play it, never a repetition — it was born this very minute. You don't say, "Oh, dawn! What else is new? This dawn is nothing but a pale replica of one I saw in my youth" — hahaha! No, because it's always *this time*. It was Mama who taught me that. The fugue is forever born anew. It goes on and on, and everything is possible.

Hey — the telephone — like last night at the same time! Is it...?

I reach the far side of the room in a single leap, press the receiver to my ear — *at birth, you were no bigger than a telephone receiver....*

"Yes?"

"Hi, sweetie!"

"Oh... hi, Papa."

"How're things?"

"All right."

"Can you put your mama on the line?"

"Uh... she went out... to buy some bread."

I'm not telling a fib. "She went out to buy some bread" is a true statement. But it's like the fugue — it doesn't mean the same thing today as it did yesterday.

"Tell her I'd like to take the two of you out to dinner tomorrow night, okay? I don't want her to bother with shopping and cooking. Could you tell her that? Your mama's a bit tired these days...."

"Yeah, I know."

"Nothing escapes your eagle-eyes, does it?"

"Nope!"

"Well... so maybe you could... sort of... pamper her a little bit tonight... okay?"

"Yeah, sure!"

"Were you... er... playing the piano?"

"Mm-hm."

"Maybe you could... stop playing now and give her a hand.... I don't know... set the table or something."

"Okay, Papa. Don't worry, I'll set the table. Bye, see you tomorrow!"

And since I don't like fibbing, I do set the table. For two — Mama and me. Maybe our ghosts will sit down and eat together in the middle of the night! Do living people have ghosts, or only dead people? So far I haven't seen Babushka's ghost... but if I did, I bet I wouldn't be scared at all!

I turn off all the lights and go up to my room.

BENJAMIN

"Maya?"

Everything's dark on the ground floor. I stand there in the hallway, holding my bag of food supplies and feeling pretty small. In the pale, ghostly light of the street lamps, the pianos and the living-room furniture look like big animals ready to pounce — personally I don't care much for big animals, I only like small ones, the smaller the better — "Maya?" — where can she be? I can hear my own voice trembling — hey, I'm the one who's supposed to protect *her*, not the other way around....

Suddenly she materializes at the top of the staircase. I can't make out her face in the half-light, all I can see is her nightgown — a narrow white rectangle — and her pointy black hair bristling up around her head. She looks like a black-and-white daisy.

"I'm up here. You coming?"

So I go upstairs. On tiptoe, which is ridiculous, since she's the only one in the house.

"Oh, great! You got away! Lucien didn't suspect anything?"

"It was a piece of cake," I tell her. "He went to bed early; he's been snoring his head off for the past hour!"

Both of us burst out laughing. I feel a lot better — now that we're in her bedroom. She's turned out all the lights except a night light, so as not to draw the neighbours' attention. Everything's really spooky and secret and dangerous, like we're a couple of accomplices in some detective movie. I'm getting into it.

"Doesn't it give you the creeps to be alone in a big house like this?" I ask, forgetting my own jitters of thirty seconds ago and playing my protector role to the hilt.

"Oh, no.... not at all."

The dragonfly sits down cross-legged on her unmade bed, and I glimpse half a dozen stuffed animals in the disarray of her sheets — she must have been feeling a *little* bit lonesome!

"Look," I say. "I raided the fridge. I brought you some stuff to eat...."

"*Wow!*"

Her eyes pop out of her head when I start taking the food out of the plastic bag: a piece of smoked sausage, a big hunk of bread, a carton of yogurt, a few cherry-plums.... She attacks it, cramming the food into her mouth so fast she hardly has time to chew it.... It makes me laugh to watch her.

"Sorry!" she says with a big yogurty smile. "Not very polite, am I?"

"You know," I say, "when you walk into a silkworm-breeding house and the worms are eating, you can hear it. Thousands of mandibles chomping on mulberry leaves at the same time... It's amazing — it sounds just like raindrops on the roof!"

"That's incredible!"

She's nice; she always appreciates my stories. Wiping her mouth with her hand, she jumps out of bed and brushes the breadcrumbs from her nightgown.

"Can you stay a while?" She glances at me sideways — almost shyly, which is not like her at all — and I can tell she'd rather I not leave right away.

"Uh... sure, why not?... Long as I'm home before my uncle wakes up."

"Wait! I'll be right back!"

She goes tearing into the next room in her bare feet, and comes back a minute later with her mother's alarm clock.

"Look! We can get up at six o'clock. Okay?"

She props up the alarm clock on her bedside table and slips into bed, scooting all the way over to the wall.

For a while I stand there like an idiot. I can feel the hairs prickling on my thighs. I'm about to sleep with a girl for the first time in my life and it feels weird . She's only ten, I tell myself. Poupette's age. It's like sleeping with your little sister. Yeah, sure. Except it's *not* like sleeping with my little sister. Not at all.

I take off my thongs and my Bermuda shorts — leave the rest on — and slip into bed next to the mosquito. She falls asleep right away — bing! Out like a light. But it takes me a long time to get to sleep. I lie there staring at Maya in the faint light, she's facing me and breathing very softly, I can see her tiny nostrils flare as the air goes through them, sweet little dragonfly, so fragile and so strong at the same time — now she stirs in her sleep, she must be dreaming... It can't go on like this, I say to myself. Nobody can fend for themselves at the age of ten. I don't like this situation. I don't want to betray her secret but.... Where the hell can her mother be?

MAYA

What's that?

Is that you, Mama?

Quick quick, I climb over Benjamin, I don't want to wake him up but — well, too bad if I do — what was that noise? The front door? Was that Mama coming home — is that you, Mama? It takes me about three seconds to get downstairs — but no — there's no one there — it must have been the wind, the wind has come up and it's making the shutters bang, maybe there's gonna be a storm, like on the day of my audition.... Remember how we ran together in the rain? You bought me a whole bunch of meringues, and by the time we got home we were soaked to the skin!

Okay. It was nothing. So I go back upstairs. Benjamin is sitting on the bed, wide awake. He looks worried. "What's wrong? Where were you?"

"Nothing, I was just thirsty. I went down to get a glass of water. Sorry. I didn't mean to wake you up."

I get back into bed, and just then it starts raining. First a few fat, scattered drops, then a violent downpour.... *Listen!... Yes, that's right, my little one, it's raining! That's right — and now the sun has come out! Tiny, iridescent droplets cling to the edges of the leaves and tremble there, a huge rainbow inside each and every one!...* We don't go back to sleep. We just lie there listening to the rain on the roof, making a noise like silkworm mandibles. I'm glad Benjamin's here.

We lie face to face, looking at each other but not talking. I'm sure we haven't fallen asleep, but suddenly the alarm goes off and we wake up with a start. We've got our arms around each other. It's already getting light.

I walk him to the door. Just as he's about to leave, I kiss him on the lips.... And then he's gone, without a word.

ROBERT

I don't believe in premonitions, but I've got a premonition. As soon as I park my car in front of the house, a sort of... well, yes, a feeling... that something's not right. Yet everything seems as usual — the high rosebushes on either side of the walkway, the grass still glistening from last night's rainfall, the sound of piano music wafting through the open windows....

Maybe it's Sofia's absence — I still haven't gotten used to it. My mother-in-law. I no longer have a mother-in-law. A whole dimension of irony, whimsicality and solid good sense has vanished from our lives...

The screen door slams behind me and the music comes to a halt. Maya runs up — leaping into my arms as she does every Saturday, wrapping her legs around my waist and planting a big, noisy kiss on my forehead... but I still can't get rid of this... unpleasant... whatever.

"Where's your Mama?"

"Uh... Mama?"

She leaps down and starts flipping through her sheet music. Why is she avoiding my eyes? What's going on?

"Mama had an adjudication at the Conservatory. She won't be home until late afternoon."

"An adjudication? In mid-August? That wasn't on her schedule, was it?"

"Sure it was," says Maya, still feverishly riffling through her music books, as though she'd lost something inside of them....

"Why didn't you tell me about it yesterday on the phone?"

"Oh, I thought you knew."

"No, I *didn't* know. And I don't see why Lara didn't tell me.... Well, anyway...." I try to shake off the absurd sensation of dark shadows hovering around my shoulders, voices whispering behind my back — it's beginning to get on my nerves.

"Have you had lunch?" I ask her.

"No. I'm not really hungry."

She goes back to the piano and I head for the kitchen.... But I practically have to force myself to put one foot in front of the other — this is insane. Good Lord, *what's going on?* What on earth could be waiting for me in the kitchen? I've always looked down on people who were superstitious....

No... the kitchen is the kitchen. Perfectly ordinary. The only false note is a vase of wilted roses on the table. Lara always throws flowers out the minute they lose their bloom; she hates to see things go bad.... I open the refrigerator. *There* I'm brought up short because it's empty. There's almost nothing in it, not even a quart of milk — I've never seen it so empty before. Maybe Lara planned on doing some food shopping on her way home from the Conservatory.... Or else she's finding it hard to buy food, now that Sofia's no longer around to make her favourite dishes....

Glancing at the roses again, I notice that exactly thirteen petals have fallen onto the table. It makes me jump, then blaze up in anger at myself for seeing it as a bad omen. Damn it, damn it to hell. I sweep the petals into the garbage can.

I'll make some spaghetti, Maya and I will stuff ourselves with spaghetti, and then we'll spend the afternoon playing games. I simply must get rid of this uneasy feeling.

I call Maya when the spaghetti is cooked, we set the table any old way and pour meat sauce straight from the jar onto our plates

— yes, now we're slumming it, having fun, that's better — I can feel the pressure in my chest letting up a bit. I show her how to use a fork to roll the spaghetti into coils on a spoon — but when I try and lift the spoon to my mouth, my spiral unwinds and I end up slurping it anyway. After a while we abandon all restraint, eating like pigs and getting meat sauce all over our clothes, Maya shrieks with laughter at the sight of her respectable Papa covered with red splotches — "You look like a vampire who's been drinking blood!" she giggles... and *wham*, the feeling returns. The dread. Inexplicable. It spoils my appetite, and I have to get up and make myself some coffee so my little girl won't notice.

Afterwards, as we're washing up together, she asks me, "How did you and Mama meet?"

"You know very well. We've told you the story a hundred times."

"Tell me again."

"Well, she was giving a concert with the orchestra, and I just happened to be in the audience. I was so mesmerized by her beauty that I didn't hear a single note she was playing."

"Because she was wearing a backless dress, is that right? Huh? Did you talk to her at intermission?"

"No. I didn't want to interfere with her concentration, so I decided to wait until the end of the concert."

"What about Mama? Was it love at first sight for her, too?"

"You'd have to ask her about that. But I have to say, with a bit more hair on my head and less fat on my tummy, I was pretty irresistible."

"What were the first words you said to her?"

"Oh, I don't remember."

"Yes you do, yes you do! I don't believe you! Tell the truth!"

"I don't know; I must have said, 'Uh, that Mozart *Concerto in D-Minor* was perfectly admirable.' Something like that. I didn't know a thing about music, but I'd memorized the programme so as to be able to compliment her afterwards."

"And what about her? What did she answer?"

"If I remember correctly, she answered by gazing into my eyes and letting a charming blush come over her cheeks. Only human beings blush, you know. So far, no one's been able to come up with a satisfactory evolutionary explanation of this sudden rush of blood to the face...."

"Don't try and change the subject. Did you kiss her that same night?"

"Young lady! Your questions are getting a bit out of place!"

"Tell me! Please, please tell me!"

"Well.... Maybe I waited until the *next* day. Yeah. I think I let her stew in doubt, anxiety and uncertainty for twenty-four hours. But not twenty-five!"

"And what did it feel like the first time you kissed her? Was it weird?"

"Hey, that's enough out of you! Aren't you supposed to be doing your arpeggios or something?"

Kissing Lara for the first time, twenty years ago.... Lara's lips, at age twenty-five.... They've changed so little, it's unbelievable.... They are still as full and soft and tender as they used to be. And as sad....

But why is everything so out of kilter today?

ALINE

At first I don't notice anything — probably because I'm running late. I promised Camille I'd pick her up at the library at three and it's already ten past, I wasted a lot of time standing in line at the cashier's, so I just sort of dive into the car with my shopping-bags, totally oblivious to the lady who's standing there....

But right afterwards, of course, I see her — as soon as I settle in behind the steering-wheel. It's impossible *not* to see her because she's standing there right in front of me, leaning against the hood of the car. Not for a second do I mistake her for a prostitute or a homeless person; it doesn't even occur to me. Partly because she's well dressed — she's wearing a stylish red cotton pantsuit... and partly because of the way she holds herself. She's not exactly sitting on the hood and she hasn't collapsed onto it either, she's just sort of *leaning* against it, as if — I don't know how else to put it — as if she hoped it might give her some sort of moral support.

I look at my watch, which is silly because I just looked at it a second ago and it still says ten past three. I think of Camille waiting for me — so I turn the key in the ignition, rather unkindly, to start the car. I expect the lady to jump a foot in the air and then move on, with hasty gestures of apology.... But that's not what happens. Nothing happens. She just stays there, in exactly the same position. So I honk the horn. Softly and repeatedly, like when you're driving through a crowd of people having a street party. She still doesn't budge. She doesn't even turn around, and I realize there's something wrong with her. At this point, Camille moves down a notch or two on my list of worries (although the librarian pointedly told me the library was not a babysitting service), and this strange woman moves up to the top.

Getting out of the car, I shut the door and walk up to her.

"Madam?"

She stares at me. She's in her forties, and there's a real air of elegance about her. Yes — just as I thought — she's anything but a homeless person. Looks more like a university professor or an aging actress.... But what strikes me the most is that... she isn't there. Her eyes are empty and her face is... harrowed. Distraught.

"Is something wrong?"

She's still staring at me, and her gaze makes my blood run cold. No one's ever looked at me that way in my life, and I hope it won't happen again. She stares at me... the way you stare at rain, from the window of a moving train. It can't be put into words — there's nothing out there but sadness, as banal as it is irrefutable. There's no possible exchange. It wouldn't occur to you to talk to the rain. You look at it, you take it in... and it drives you to despair, that's all.

I have no idea what to do next. I know a little bit about psychology, but suffering that closes you in behind walls like that is... beyond me. The woman needs professional care, that much is obvious. And that moment of looking into each other's eyes — mine sympathetic, hers bleak, dead — marks the beginning of a series of events which will land her behind real walls.

I step into the nearest café and ask for someone to call the police.

Then I walk out of this woman's life, as discreetly and as arbitrarily as I had walked into it.

I'll never know who she was.

ROBERT

I sit on the back porch and read the newspaper, while Maya works away at her dear old Gibbons. We've spent countless afternoons like this, there's nothing unusual about it — yet when the telephone rings, it sets my brain on fire. I know beyond a shadow of a doubt that within the next few minutes, my spark of premonition is going to flare up into a catastrophe.

Maya must know it, too, because upon hearing the phone ring she breaks off playing and rushes over to answer it — something she never usually does when there's a parent around. She listens for a moment; then I see her face light up.

"They've found Mama!" she cries out triumphantly, handing me the receiver. (Ah? so she knew Lara was lost?)

From then on, I have the uncanny sense of being an actor in a play, pronouncing lines written for me, ages in advance, by a sadistic author. I say that yes, I am indeed Monsieur Mestral. Yes. Lara Mestral's husband (and in a sense, I've never been as much her husband as

I am today). I answer a number of other facile, factual questions. And finally, I jot down the address of the hospital to which she's been taken.

MAYA

Mama!

Oh, I'm so happy to see you! Everything will be all right now, you'll see. I'll come and visit you every day. My Mamochka... I love you, you know. You don't have to talk if you don't feel like it. It's all right. I understand. Look, I'll cover your hands with kisses, I'll take you in my arms. I'll tell you a thousand million stories!

ROBERT

Once the formalities of the transfer from hospital to clinic have been taken care of, I leave Maya alone with her mother and go out into the corridor, to discuss the situation with the psychiatrist. I can't rid myself of the feeling that we've regressed to ten years ago. Here we are in the white room again — no windows, nothing but artificial light. And here are the white-clad doctors and nurses, their rapid steps in the hallway, their whispered confabulations, heads tipped to one side, eyes filled with fear.

A return to the beginning — dawn again — square one, with mental patients in lieu of premature babies. More limbo. More anxiety. Random phrases scrawled and scribbled in the margins of the page, outside the limits of the officially worded, neatly printed text.

Lara is exceptionally peaceful. She's aware of our presence, she recognizes us, there's no doubt about that — but she doesn't talk anymore. The psychiatrist, anxious to protect himself from what will always be a mystery, namely the unspeakable contortions of the human soul, tells me the name of her pathology in his jargon. If I understand correctly, what it comes down to is mental exhaustion. So what else is new?

He says that Lara will need a prolonged sleeping cure; that she is already under heavy sedation.

No wonder she's so peaceful.

MAYA

You're me, you're my mother! No matter what you do, I'll never leave you. Don't talk, if you don't feel like it. Take your time. I'm not afraid of silence — you're the one who showed me how beautiful it can be, and how important it is to music. You *are* music, my Mamochka, so no wonder you should need silence, every now and then. Have some! Have as much as you like.

I'm here with you. *When you breathe in, my lungs fill up with air; when you laugh, my heart leaps for joy.* Oh, I know — you're not really up to laughing as yet, but it won't be long now. You can count on me. I'll come to visit you every day without fail. I'll talk to you, and.... we'll come through this together, I promise you.

This is a nice clinic you're in, you know? I'd never even seen this neighbourhood before. There're lots of big trees in the garden — mostly chestnut trees. It isn't even autumn yet and their leaves are already starting to turn. I like it when they turn. Before they get all brown and shrivelly, a yellow pattern appears on the green. Each leaf has a different pattern — it's like there were a million little abstract paintings up there!

MAYA

Yesterday I went over to Lucien's place. He was wrapping up his three little saints to take them out to the church that ordered them. It's not too far from town — about an hour's drive, he says — we'll go see them together when you get out. He was so proud of the final result — you should have seen him! He says you never know how a stained-glass window's going to turn out. For weeks you work in the dark. You do the painting, the firing, the mounting, the soldering, the puttying... but until you put the thing in place, you have no idea what the effect is going to be.... He says it's like a pregnancy, like when you've got a little baby growing in the dark. All you can do is wait, and hope that everything will be all right, and then at the end... hey, that's *fantastic!* Lucien said to give you a great big hug. He asks about you every day. He's jealous because I've got visiting permission and he doesn't.... He really loves you, Mamochka. Me too. Just wait and see, I'll show you how strong my love is!....

Benjamin showed me his box of silkworms again — and, just as he'd predicted, the ones we didn't kill have turned into butterflies. Boy, are they ugly! He warned me in advance but still, I couldn't help being surprised how ugly they are, coming out of such beautiful silk cocoons!

Benjamin goes home the day after tomorrow, and I head back to school — sixth grade, can you *believe* it? And a couple of weeks from now, Papa will take me to Berlin for my first lesson with Dianescu. I'll tell you all about it, I promise. Every little detail. I'll tell you if he picks his nose or if he leaves his cell phone on during lessons.... Anyway, no matter how good a teacher he is, he could never be a better one than you; that would be impossible. Oh yeah, I forgot — your students keep calling up to ask how you're feeling. And lots of your colleagues from the Conservatory. Everybody says you should get a good rest and come home as soon as you can — they miss you!

I'm listening to you Mama. You know that? Even if you think you're not talking, I'm listening to you as hard as I can. Real musicians know how to decipher silence; you're the one who taught me that. You taught me *everything I know and everything I don't know about music, the eighty-eight notes of the keyboard and the hundred million constellations in the sky, every note a star — including you, yes, a star, my little star–* I need you, Mamochka!

MAYA

I sure hope they're nice to you here. I hope they take good care of you.... Papa's a pretty lousy cook. The only thing he knows how to make without flubbing it is spaghetti. But he does his best, you've got to give him that. Last night he tried to make lamb stew and it was completely inedible, but who cares? At least he doesn't mind my teasing him....

Remember all the wonderful dishes Babushka made for us? Remember her stuffed cabbage and her cabbage soup and her pickled cabbage and her grated cabbage and her cabbage blintzes and her braised cabbage? Remember how the kitchen stank of garlic because of her heart concoctions? Remember how she used to say: *Dis ting is good!* and we'd burst out laughing and hold our noses: *Yeah, the stink is good!*

Do you miss your Mamochka? Are you sad she died? Don't be sad, Mama.... Children are put on earth to comfort their parents. Lucien told me about the next little saint he wants to make — her name was Paule-Elisabeth something or other, she was Italian. When she turned twenty her parents married her off to a sixty-year-old count who had a passion for music. So every night for the next eighteen years, he forced her to attend these boring concerts — she thought she'd go out of her mind! She had three children, but two of them died young and her husband was so jealous of the third one, Charles, that she had to send him away to school. Finally the husband died. But then, shortly afterwards, so did the son. Paule-Elisabeth wept so bitterly at his bedside that Charles came to comfort her.

"Don't worry," he said, "God will send you more children." She found that pretty hard to believe, but it's exactly what happened — she started adopting little orphan-girls. First two of them, then two more, and two more, and before long there were hundreds of them, her castle was swarming with little girls — Lucien's stained glass window is going to be just fantastic, with all the little girls swinging from the chandeliers and sliding down the bannisters!

...When he got to the part about the boring concerts, it reminded me of the story of Ivan and his magic violin that Babushka told me once. I must have fallen asleep before she got to the end. I remember how Ivan makes Master Penny-Pincher furious by forcing him to dance in the thorn-bushes, but I have no idea what happens next....

Speaking of thorns, your roses are doing fine. Some of them have started getting ready for the winter — they scattered all their petals like fireworks — but gently, without a sound. They're waiting for you, Mama. So are your delphiniums. They don't mind waiting. What's the hurry? *At that rate, music goes nowhere fast!* That's what Babushka used to say, when I played something too quickly. *There's one right tempo and only one*, she used to say.

MAYA

Hey, it's cold in here! They must have set the air conditioning too high. Pretty soon, my nose and fingers will be sprouting icicles.... Why don't we go on a trip together... to some tropical country? Like India... or Zanzibar... We could go all the way to the antipodes...! Antipode and Arthropode went out on the deep blue sea....

You still don't feel like laughing, Mama?

What does *pode* mean, anyway? Look, I brought a dictionary with me today. Every single word in the language is in here — all you've got to do is look them up. *Look. Please — hang on — look!*

Let's see... pod, pod, podophtalmus: *having eyes located at the top of a peduncle*. Okay, yeah, I get it... Benjamin told me about this fly in New Guinea — the Rothschild something-or-other, it's called... The males have pedunculated eyes as long as their whole bodies; they use them to intimidate each other. The flies with short peduncles are scared of the flies with long peduncles — they take to their heels the minute they see one coming.... Men are really dumb sometimes, don't you think?

Can you hear me, Mamochka? Can you hear it when I speak to you? You're there, aren't you? You're not going to die, are you?

Let's see.... mmm... do you know what a *manticore* is? No? I'll tell you. It's a chimera or mythological beast found in India: part man, part tiger and part scorpion.... Isn't that great? Even things that *don't* exist are in the dictionary.... How about if we made up some up other chimeras? Like... uh... the *doncamoct*. A cross between a donkey, a camel and an octopus. No, that's not so good.... Wait.... I've got one. The *dramosilk*: part dragonfly, part mosquito and part silkworm! Wouldn't that be cute? Oh, Mamochka, I'm your little chimera and I love you with all my heart....

Please wake up.... I know you're not asleep but wake up anyway, I can't stand seeing you like this — please talk to me, Mama. I need you. Please, look at me, come back to me.... Wake up, I beseech you... *Wake up!!*

DOCTOR FABIEN

"How are we today, Madame Mestral?.... Well, I have some excellent news for you: your daughter is out of danger. She has reached term plus two weeks, her weight is quite acceptable, and she's beautifully coordinating the three basic activities — sucking, swallowing, and breathing."

"...Chi...mera...."

"Mara? I thought her name was Maya! Anyway, from this day onward, she should be able to start leading a normal existence. I have to admit I wasn't sure things would turn out quite so well. But she clearly made up her mind to hang on for dear life... and it's in large part thanks to you — your presence at her side, the constant encouragement you gave her. I can tell you now that not many mothers would have your courage, in such difficult circumstances...

"My sincere congratulations, Madame Mestral. You can take your baby home with you. Barring unforeseen developments, there is nothing more to worry about."

This book was set with
Janson Text, Galliard and Hoefler Text fonts.